Yours Truly,

Lucy B. PARKER

Take My Advice!

"So, girls, start thinking of who you want to ask to the dance," Dr. Rem-Wall went on.

I knew who I was asking—NO ONE. I needed to figure out how to get out of this. Maybe I would start getting really, really sick about four days before the dance, so by the time it arrived, I would still be contagious with whatever the sickness was. (Strep throat or bronchitis sounded believable. Malaria, which was a deadly disease you got from mosquitoes in the jungle, did not.)

But the more I thought about it, the more I realized that getting sick wouldn't work. I'd still have to ask someone, before I could claim sickness. The only way to really pull this off was if I pretended to break, or at least seriously sprain, my ankle or foot, way in advance. That way I could use the excuse that because I wouldn't be able to dance, it wouldn't be worth me asking anyone because it would be unfair for whoever I asked to just have to sit there with me on the bleachers the entire night.

I needed a plan. And fast.

Yours Truly,

Take My Advice!

ROBIN PALMER

PUFFIN BOOKS
An Imprint of Penguin Group (USA) Inc.

PUFFIN BOOKS
Published by the Penguin Group
Penguin Young Readers Group, 345 Hudson Street,
New York, New York 10014, U.S.A.
Penguin Group (Canada), 90 Eglinton Avenue East, Suite 700, Toronto,
Ontario, Canada M4P 2Y3 (a division of Pearson Penguin Canada Inc.)
Penguin Books Ltd, 80 Strand, London WC2R 0RL, England
Penguin Ireland, 25 St Stephen's Green, Dublin 2, Ireland
(a division of Penguin Books Ltd)
Penguin Group (Australia), 250 Camberwell Road, Camberwell,
Victoria 3124, Australia (a division of Pearson Australia Group Pty Ltd)
Penguin Books India Pvt Ltd, 11 Community Centre,
Panchsheel Park, New Delhi - 110 017, India
Penguin Group (NZ), 67 Apollo Drive, Rosedale,
Auckland 0632, New Zealand (a division of Pearson New Zealand Ltd)
Penguin Books (South Africa) (Pty) Ltd, 24 Sturdee Avenue,
Rosebank, Johannesburg 2196, South Africa

Registered Offices: Penguin Books Ltd, 80 Strand,
London WC2R 0RL, England

First published in the United States of America by Puffin Books and
G. P. Putnam's Sons, divisions of Penguin Young Readers Group, 2012

1 3 5 7 9 10 8 6 4 2

LIBRARY OF CONGRESS CATALOGING-IN-PUBLICATION DATA IS AVAILABLE

Puffin Books ISBN 978-0-14-241503-0

Printed in the United States of America

ALWAYS LEARNING   PEARSON

For Kaitlyn McNab,
and her glorious Kaitlynness

Yours Truly,

Lucy B. PARKER

Take My Advice!

chapter 1

Dear Dr. Maude,

Surprise—it's me! I bet you thought that because you haven't heard from me in a while, I had gone away, huh? You know, because you never responded to ANY of the 33 e-mails I've sent you? Nope. Still here.

Once when I was overlistening to my mom (as I think I've mentioned, she calls it eavesdropping, but I find that to be a really ugly word), I heard her say that sometimes I have trouble taking a hint. But while some people may look at that as a bad thing—like something you'd find in the "Needs Improvement" section of your report card—I happen to think it's a very positive quality.

For instance, the way that Cristina Pollock was all "Who does that new girl Lucy B. Parker think she is, running for class president against me, the most popular girl in the seventh grade at the Center for Creative Learning?" Now most kids after hearing that would take the hint and drop out of the race. Especially if there were other hints as well— say, if incredibly embarrassing photos of them, where they look like an egghead due to a bad haircut after an incident with a straightening iron, were blown up to poster size and plastered on the walls during the campaign. Or a video made up of blooper photo moments of that person was shown to the entire school until the principal ordered it taken down. But if you haven't figured it out yet, I'm not like most kids.

Maybe it's because between the Straightening Iron Incident and the Hat Incident (where I was completely humiliated when the director of my then-enemy-now-frister Laurel Moses's movie pulled off my hat so everyone in Northampton, Massachusetts, saw my almost-bald head), I'm just used to humiliation. Not only did Cristina Pollock's meanness and her threats not stop me from running, but I WON THE ELECTION and am now the official seventh-grade class president. Which is something that wouldn't have happened if I had gotten the hint and just continued to let her dork discriminate me and remain a Have while I stayed a Have-Not.

Anyway, to make a long story short, that's why you haven't heard from me. Because I'm super-busy. I have to meet with the presidents of all the after-school clubs. (Kevin Rudnick from the Reptile Club can whine all he wants, but as long as I'm in office, there is NOT going to be a Bring-Your-Reptile-to-School Day because that's just plain gross.) And I organized a Fix-Your-Bad-Karma-Now Food Drive to collect food for the homeless. (As I've told you, I'm really into making sure my karma is good. Who wouldn't want extra-credit-like points for good behavior in this life to bring into your next one when you're reincarnated?)

Seriously, I barely have any time to go do fun stuff after

school. Like I never get to play TWUO (The World's Ugliest Outfit) with Alice, Malia, and Beatrice at Strawberry's on Broadway and 72nd street anymore. (Alice always wins because like Marissa, my sort-of friend back in Northampton, she's just naturally drawn to ugly clothes. Especially if they're yellow or have sequins or rhinestones on them.)

In fact, I'm so busy that I barely have the energy to stay awake and watch the episodes of your show *Come On, People—Get with the Program* that I TiVo every day. (Although I did catch the one on hoarding with the woman who had every issue of the *New York Times* going back to 1982. That was AWESOME. My mom thinks hoarders are beyond creepy, but I LOVE them. Although because I love animals so much, I can't watch that show *Animal Hoarders* on Animal Planet.)

Well, I have to go now. It's time for my weekly Skype session with my brother Ziggy. Because he's only a month old, it's just me talking while he lies there like a potato, but I don't mind. Sometimes it's nice to have a conversation where no one is interrupting you every two seconds with dumb questions (like Alice) that, if they would just let you FINISH your sentence, they would find out the answer.

I know it sounds weird, but I'm pretty sure Ziggy understands what I'm talking about. For instance, the last time we Skyped, when I asked him if he thought the fact that Blair Lerner-Moskovitz (my sort-of-but-not-entirely-official-because-I'm-too-afraid-to-tell-his-sister-aka-my-BFF-Beatrice crush) wasn't grossed out by how I like to put grape jelly on my hamburgers was a sign that maybe he liked me, I swear he nodded. Dad said that sometimes when Ziggy's passing gas, it can look like a nod, but this was more of a nod-nod.

Oh—BTW—remember how I was nervous about him being born because I was afraid that he'd get all the attention and Dad would love him more than me and forget I existed? Well, that hasn't been the case. In fact, if anything, I give ZIGGY a ton of attention and end up ignoring DAD a little because every time we talk on the phone I spend most of the conversation asking about Ziggy. Obviously, things could be different when Ziggy becomes an actual person rather than just a lump of a baby. I mean, for all I know, he could end up becoming completely annoying like Beatrice is always saying Blair is, but at the moment, it's really cool. Especially since I'm no longer afraid I'm going to drop him or mistakenly push on the soft spot on his head so that his brains fall out like Marissa told me could happen.

After Ziggy and I Skype, I have to go write my weekly update for the school paper. Beatrice says I should just do it on video, like the president does, but while that would be a way for me to spend more time with Blair on account of the fact that he's our official Video Guy, I don't want to have to worry about my bloversharing (that's blurting plus oversharing) problem kicking up. Now that I've gotten to know him better, I'm a little less nervous around him, but I don't want to take any chances. I mean, what if, by mistake, I just HAPPEN to mention the fact that I'm really mad that I STILL haven't gotten my period? (BTW, I'm seriously considering sending away for this special powder you sprinkle into orange juice that I saw advertised in the back of a magazine. It's supposed to make it appear within 24 hours or your money back, but then in tiny letters at the bottom I noticed it said "Please be advised that your money may not necessarily be returned in U.S. dollars but may come in another form of foreign currency such as Tanzanian schillings." Which, if that were the case, would mean I wouldn't be able to use the money unless I went to Tanzania, and, as much as I'd like to go because it's in Africa with very interesting wildlife, I have no plans to do in the near future.)

There is one thing that I wanted to ask you about. Why I think this will be the e-mail you finally respond to, I don't know, but I figured I'll give it a try. Anyway, it has to do with Alan, my stepfather. (Because he and Mom can't decide on a place to get married, he's not technically my stepfather yet, but because we already live together and have official family dinners, it's easier to call him that.) Even though he's super-organized and constantly scheduling things into his BlackBerry like "10:15—Sit down and make sure BlackBerry schedule is up to date," I love him a lot. And now that we've all lived together for six months, I feel like he's calmed down and is less worried about how our family is going to blend. That's a good thing because it means his hands don't get all clammy anymore. Which, when he forces me to hold his hand when we cross the street during our IBSs (Individual Bonding Sessions), even though I keep telling him that I'm way too old to be holding a parent's hand as we cross the street, is helpful.

But lately I've started to feel that he's kind of disappointed in me. Like the more he gets to know me, the more he realizes that I'm just a normal, average kid. Meaning I get okay-but-not-amazing grades in school (especially in math, which you know I hate). And my coordination issue makes it difficult for me to find hobbies that other girls my age do, like ballet or gymnastics. And because I have such a bad singing voice that Ms. Edut, my chorus teacher back in Northampton, made me mouth the words during our holiday pageant, it's not like I can do anything music-related.

So on the one hand, there's Laurel—his REAL daughter—who's this ginormous superstar with a hit TV show who's such a good singer that she's had number one hits . . . and then there's me. Regular old Lucy B. Parker, whose biggest talent seems to be the fact that she can touch her nose with her tongue.

Sure, I won the school election and all, but the other day when I was overlistening to him and Mom, I heard him say that while he's glad I'm class president, he'd like to see me involved in more after-school activities. According to him, you need stuff like that on your school record if you want to get into a good college. I don't know why he's talking about college when I'm only in middle school. I almost said that to him, but if I had, he would have known I was overlistening, and then Mom would've yelled at me.

When we say good night, he always says "Good night,

Lucy. I love you," (Rule number 14 of the Official Parker-Moses Family Rule Book: Every family member must say good night to all other family members, even if it's via text because one of the family members is on location shooting a movie.) But sometimes I wonder if he only says that because he HAS to love me, because he loves my mom.

If you had any advice about what you think I could do to make it so that he's just as proud of me as he is of Laurel, I'd appreciate it.

yours truly,
LUCY B. PARKER

P.S. Not to alarm you or anything, but you know Dr. David? That guy whose show *Be the Best You That You Can Be!* is on the same time as yours? Well, I just happened to catch a little bit of it the other day, and I have to say, it was very inspiring. And in the part I caught, he mentioned that he reads and answers EVERY SINGLE E-MAIL that he receives. Not that I'm planning on writing to him or anything. But I'm just saying.

Beatrice said I was overreacting about the hobby thing, but I wasn't. Because a few nights later, during one of our official family dinners, Alan handed out a photocopied article to Mom, Laurel, and me.

"Another article?" Laurel asked. "Is there going to be a quiz on it?"

I looked at her and tried not to laugh. If the paparazzi had somehow managed to get past Pete, our doorman, and up to our apartment on the twenty-first floor and snapped a picture of her, it would've been a disaster. Because she had a big scene to shoot the next day and wanted to look her best, her long blonde hair had deep conditioner in it and was under a shower cap, and she had zit medicine dotted all over her face. Definitely not what you'd expect to see the most famous girl in America looking like.

Not to sound full of myself, but, *I*, on the other hand, was looking good. A year after the Straightening Iron Incident, my brown hair had grown to the point where, while not exactly *long*, certainly couldn't be called *short*. Plus, because Roger—Laurel's, and now *my*, personal hairdresser—was so good, he had managed to cut it in such a way than it looked longer than it really was. Not only that, but I had recently come across these V-neck sweaters at Old Navy that managed to make my boobs look a lot smaller, so I convinced Mom to buy them in all seven colors and was now wearing the red one. That, with my new denim jeggings and purple cowboy boots (scored during one of my IBSs with Laurel at a thrift store in Chelsea) had become my favorite outfit. I had decided that if Blair ever ended up asking me to do something, that's what I was going to wear.

"No, no quiz," Alan replied. After the article about global warming that he had handed out a few weeks ago during a Current Events–themed dinner, he had quizzed us the next day to test our comprehension skills. Luckily, we weren't being graded, because I had totally screwed up. Instead of listening and comprehending, I was busy thinking about what I'd wear if for any reason the red sweater and jeggings happened to be in the wash on the day that Blair and I hung out. *If* we ever hung out. "Just thought there was some interesting stuff here."

Mom reached over and stroked the small amount of hair he had left as he slowly went bald. "Oh honey—I love how you always find a way to make meals educational!"

I squinted at her to see if she was making fun of him, but she was serious. I could tell because her blue eyes got all crinkly. But then again, because she was forty-seven, they were at the point where they were getting crinkly (or wrinkly) even when she wasn't smiling. She was also getting more gray, but thanks to Roger, that part wasn't too noticeable in her brown hair.

"*Studies show that children with hobbies are not only happier, but are at a lower risk for heart disease,*" I read aloud. I looked up. "So because I don't have any hobbies I'm going to get sick?!"

"Of course not," Mom assured me before she scanned the article. "Hmm. This is interesting. It says that the serotonin levels in children who play an instrument and have some sort of creative outlet are much higher than those whose primary form of recreation is watching television."

I had no idea what serotonin meant, but I didn't like the sound of it. "What does that mean?" I asked suspiciously.

"Serotonin is this chemical in your brain that makes you feel happy," Laurel explained. Because so much of being an actress was about waiting around in your trailer or dressing room waiting to act, Laurel read a lot. And not just novels or teen magazines or *US Weekly*, but important grown-up magazines, like *Time* and *Newsweek*.

"So the article is saying that I'm sad because I like to watch TV?" I asked nervously.

"Not exactly," Mom replied, while at the same time Alan said "Exactly."

Uh-oh. We were having an UBFM—Unblended Blended Family Moment. That was when even though for the most part a blended family was getting along really well and there wasn't a lot of "your mom this" and "your dad that" stuff, something happened where it became clear that the parents were on opposite sides of the fence about something. Then you had to sit there awkwardly while they figured it out, hoping that your parent wasn't the one who caved and let the other one win, which then ended up with you getting the short end of the stick on something. Like, say, being told you couldn't watch TV anymore.

"Well, it's not saying you're . . . *sad*," Alan corrected. "It's just saying that you'd feel more fulfilled if you had some other kind of hobbies. Like piano. Or . . . Girl Scouts."

I shook my head. "Not going to happen." We had been through this a bunch of times. I was *so* not a Girl Scout girl. Not only wasn't I good at crafts, but the one time I had tried on Marissa's blechy green uniform back in Northampton, it was super-itchy.

For a while I thought maybe overlistening could be my hobby, but while I loved our apartment here in New York, I didn't get to practice it as much as I did back in Northampton. It had been a lot easier to overlisten at our old house, on account of the fact that I knew exactly what stair to stand on to both (a) hear, and (b) not get caught. Our apartment here in New York may have been big compared to most people's ("You know, Lucy," Pete was always saying, "for a lotta people in New York, their kitchens are in their *living rooms!*"), but it wasn't big enough for me not to get busted. Some people's mothers say they have eyes in the back of their head, but mine had ears in the back of hers. ("Lucy B. Parker—I can hear you *breathing*! And if you don't stop eavesdropping right this second, I'm going to go into that closet of yours and take all those boxes of maxipads and pantiliners and throw them in the garbage!" was one of her favorite threats.)

"Plus, TV is very educational and makes you well rounded," I added. "Especially the shows on Animal Planet where they go to Africa."

Laurel nodded. "She's right."

I smiled at her. That was one of the best things about having a frister (friend + sister, and a much nicer-sounding word than stepsister)—there was always someone to back you up. Unless you were having a "your mom this"/"your dad that" moment.

I pointed to my cat, Miss Piggy, who was lying at my feet waiting for me to drop some food on the floor. For the most part she didn't like me too much, but when it came to meals, she was my BFF because my coordination problem meant I dropped food a lot. "And I like to spend time with animals myself. That's a hobby." Okay, maybe I was stretching the truth a bit. Maybe some particular animals hissed when you tried to snuggle them and meowed nonstop when you tried to lock them in your room so you could spend quality time with them. But even if it wasn't a hobby of Miss Piggy's, it could still be mine.

"And that's all really great, Lucy," Alan said. "It's just that those kinds of things don't make a lot of difference on school transcripts when it comes time to applying to colleges—"

"Honey, why don't we talk about something else?" Mom asked gently. She knew that having to talk about college when I was only in middle school freaked me out and made my stomach hurt.

Alan shrugged. "Okay." He scrolled down the agenda. "Well, in the Important Announcements and Reminders section, I just want to remind everyone that in three weeks, Rebecca and I will be going away to celebrate our one-year anniversary."

Laurel and I kicked each other under the table at the same time. We knew what that meant: adults going away = them Doing It in hotel rooms = BEYOND GROSS.

"Did you decide where you're going?" asked Laurel.

"Somewhere in the country," Mom said.

"Somewhere in the city," Alan said at the same time.

They looked at each other and sighed. As much as Mom and Alan had realized they had in common when playing the I-Can't-Believe-You-Like-That-Too! game the first time we all went out for dinner together, they were also opposite in a lot of ways. Like, say, the fact that Mom finds hikes in nature very relaxing, while Alan finds them very stressful because of all the bugs. And the idea that Alan was usually seven and a half minutes early for every appointment, whereas Mom was fifteen minutes late because, even with the hook Alan had put up for her near the front door with the big sign that said REBECCA'S KEYS she still managed to misplace them. Mom said it was okay to be different in some ways because of the whole "opposites attract" thing, but it sure seemed to make planning weekends away difficult.

"We're still working on it," she said.

I was sorry they were having trouble, but if it took Alan's mind off the fact that my only extracurricular activities were watching TV and eating cupcakes, I was okay with it.

After our weekly assembly at school that Friday afternoon, I had a lot more to worry about than if Alan thought I was just taking up space in the apartment with my averageness.

As always, the assembly was super-boring, with our principal, Dr. Remington-Wallace, aka Dr. Rem-Wall, going on and on about things no one really cared about, like the signed copies of the new book *How to Become a Math Lover* by her cousin Stanley Frisson that were for sale in the office. Which, as far as I was concerned, was a total waste of paper because everyone knew that nothing short of a math hater having a brain transplant could do that.

It was 2:07, that point in the day where absolutely no one was paying attention other than the total butt kissers like Lydia Hudson and Jared Levine. Because of the seventh-grade class-president thing, I had to sit on the stage with the presidents of the other grades, which meant that not only did I have to look like I was paying attention, but I also had to look like I found what Dr. Rem-Wall was saying was interesting. At least I had my Bonne Bell Coconut Lip Smacker to keep me going. It was so yummy that if I pretended hard enough, as I slathered it on my lips, I could almost convince myself that instead of listening to Dr. Rem-Wall go on and on about math, I was at home at my kitchen table making my way through a slice of coconut cream cake. I had recently realized that Lip Smackers didn't just make your lips soft—they were also a good snack substitute if no actual snacks were available at the moment.

Other than Jared and Lydia, no one in the audience was paying attention. They were either drawing on their arm (Malia), twirling their hair around their finger and getting it stuck in their ring (Beatrice), admiring themselves in the tiny mirror that they brought with them everywhere (Cristina Pollock), or staring into space and drooling (Mitchell Fries).

That is, until the Announcement. After that, things got nuts.

"And before we dismiss you for the weekend, I have an announcement to make," said Dr. Rem-Wall. Before she went on, she tapped the microphone really hard, which is what she liked to do to make sure we'd hear what she said next, but instead it split our eardrums. "And that is, I'm pleased to announce that because of an overwhelming amount of suggestions in the suggestion box, for the first time in the history of the Center for Creative Learning, the seventh grade will be able to attend the Sadie Hawkins dance this month—"

As a tidal wave of gasps rose from the audience, I stood up. "Wait a minute—*what*?!" I yelled. Not very presidential of me, but if this was true, this was not good. In fact, this was very, very bad.

"Lucy, I *knew* you were wrong when you said that

Dr. Rem-Wall just threw away the suggestions from the suggestion box without even reading them!" Alice yelled from the audience.

I plopped back into my chair and slunk down as Dr. Rem-Wall gave me a look. It wasn't Alice's fault that she was deaf in one ear, which made her talk REALLY loud. Or that once I had taught her to overlisten, she had learned that, according to her mom, she was an "overexcitable type." But stuff like that did not earn her points on the second-non-frister-BFF front.

"OMIGOD, THIS IS THE BEST NEWS EVER!" she screeched. Why was it that all really annoying people screeched? My friend Marissa back in Northampton screeched, too. And why did they jump up and down in their seats like they were in the audience of a game show and had just gotten called up on stage?

Best news ever? Try the *worst* news ever. Ever since Beatrice had told me about the eighth-grade Sadie Hawkins dance during our first official friend get-together at Billy's Bakery back in April, I had been dreading getting older, even though getting older meant that at some point I'd have to get my period. (Although if I didn't get it until I was sixteen, which, when I Googled "do some girls just NEVER get their periods," was something I had read happened, I was going to be REALLY mad.)

We didn't have Sadie Hawkins dances back in Northampton, Massachusetts, where I had lived for my entire life until Mom fell in love with Alan. According to

Beatrice, Sadie Hawkins was like the first woman to ask a man out ever, so in honor of her, the girls had to ask the boys to be their dates. (Later on when I Googled her, I found out that, actually, Sadie Hawkins wasn't real—she was a made-up character in an old comic strip. But because I didn't know Beatrice very well yet and I had no other friends in New York at that point other than Laurel and Pete, I didn't bring that up in case she got all mad and embarrassed, which is what some people tend to do when you tell them they're wrong.)

I'm sorry, but why would someone want to *dance* with a boy? Most of them smelled gross from far away to begin with, so to be up close to them and have that smell actually get on your clothes? Yuck. Plus, I wasn't even sure what you did when you danced. Did you talk? Did you look at each other? Or did you just move your feet around looking at the floor while trying not to breathe on them in case you had recently had a piece of pepperoni pizza and hadn't had a chance to brush your teeth?

As far as I was concerned, boys were overrated. Why would you spend your time totally obsessing over them (like how Laurel did about fellow superstar Austin Mackenzie before he became her boyfriend back in June) when it could be spent doing things that were a lot more interesting. Like making crank calls. Or trying to get the people at the Hell's Kitchen Flea Market to sell you things like old cowboy boots for less money than they were asking for. (Although Laurel's germ phobia had gotten a lot better since I had come into her life, she still thought that the idea that anyone would wear used shoes was disgusting. But since I had done it a bunch of times and had never gotten anything gross like athlete's foot, I disagreed.)

The only reason I was bothering to come up with a crush was because, according to Beatrice, everyone was supposed to have three of them: a local one, a long distance/vacation one, and a celebrity one. We didn't have the three-crush rule back in Northampton, but it was very big in New York City. So much so that I decided that it was log-worthy and started the *Official Crush Log of the Girls at the Center for Creative Learning* to go along with my *Official Period Log of the Girls at the Center for Creative Learning* . And because it looked weird for the Keeper of the Crushes not to have her own picks in there, I had to come up with some.

It was taking me a long time to find a local crush on account of the fact that most of the boys at our school were either (a) gross, (b) obnoxious, or (c) had already been picked by a bunch of girls already. Which is why, after a lot of thought, I had decided on Blair, even though Beatrice was always saying her brother was bourgeois. (Because Beatrice planned on living in Paris when she grew up, she liked to use French words whenever she could. Even though I still wasn't sure she knew what they meant.) She also thought he was obnoxious, annoying, gross, and a know-it-all.

Other than the know-it-all thing, I hadn't noticed those other qualities in Blair. But since moving to New York and living with Laurel and Alan, I had learned firsthand that you didn't really know a person until you lived with them. For instance, as perfect and superstarry as Laurel may have looked to the rest of the world, no one but me knew that she was a little weird and nerdy thanks to her fear of germs, and the fact that she was so into organization that her favorite two events of the year were the half-yearly Container Store sales.

"So, girls, start thinking of who you want to ask to the dance," Dr. Rem-Wall went on.

I knew who I was asking—NO ONE. Even if I did finally get up the guts to tell Beatrice that Blair was my crush, I was *not* asking him to the dance. I needed to figure out how to get out of this. Maybe I would start getting really, really sick about four days before the dance, so by the time it arrived, I would still be contagious with whatever the sickness was. (Strep throat or bronchitis sounded believable. Malaria, which was a deadly disease you got from mosquitoes in the jungle, did not.)

But the more I thought about it, the more I realized that getting sick wouldn't work. I'd still have to ask someone, before I could claim sickness. The only way to really pull this off was if I pretended to break, or at least seriously sprain, my ankle or foot, way in advance. That way I could use the excuse that because I wouldn't be able to dance, it wouldn't be worth me asking anyone because it would be unfair for whoever I asked to just have to sit there with me on the bleachers the entire night.

I needed a plan. And fast.

At least I wasn't the only one who needed advice about this Sadie Hawkins thing. All my friends did. And while I may not have been able to figure out what to do about my own situation—like, say, how to hurt my foot in such a way that it didn't hurt too much and I could still walk without crutches—I was pretty good when it came to helping them with their problems. Turns out all the time I had spent after school watching Dr. Maude had paid off.

Not only that, but because I had been keeping a notebook called *Important Pieces of Advice*, I had a lot of advice already available to me. Some of the stuff in there was kind of boring (from Rose, our housekeeper: "If you spill something on yourself, try dabbing—not DRENCHING, but dabbing—a little club soda on it"). Or only good for New Yorkers (from Pete: "If you get on the subway and realize you've gotten in an un-air-conditioned car, make sure you jump off and get into one with air-conditioning because it gets real stinky real fast"). But other bits were very interesting (based on my own experience: "The idea of fighting with a friend or a frister—that's a combination of sister and friend—might be really scary, but it can actually bring you a lot closer because [a] you get to get your feelings out and [b] when it's over, you get to find out that the other person is still there").

A few days after the assembly, we were sitting at our lunch table in Alaska. Not literally the state Alaska. Everyone just called that part of the cafeteria that because it was the northernmost point, and it was where the Have-Nots sat. Even after winning the election and trying my best to make all students into Haves, I still ended up sitting on the outskirts of the cafeteria with all the other Have-Nots. I turned to Malia. "So did you do the homework assignment I gave you on Saturday?"

She nodded.

While filling up on candy at Dylan's Candy Bar over on the east side Saturday afternoon, Beatrice, Alice, and I had decided that Malia should ask Sam Meltzer to the dance on account of the fact that he was the least annoying out of the five boys who acted like they liked her in that I'm-a-boy-so-I-can't-REALLY-act-like-I-like-you-because-my-friends-would-tease-me-about-it-but-I-really-do way. Malia said she would've asked him if there was the slightest chance he wouldn't completely laugh in her face, but because she was sure he would, she didn't want to risk it.

Luckily, I remembered an old Dr. Maude episode about this woman who had been married for twenty-five years who, every morning when she woke up, was scared that that was going to be the day that her husband would turn to her and say, "I don't want to be married to you

anymore, so I'm taking Fluffy, the cat, and moving out."
Dr. Maude made her make a Reality List of all of the facts
about the situation—the being-married-twenty-five-
years thing; the fact that every night before they went to
sleep he turned to her and said, "I'm the luckiest man in
the world"; the week before he had talked about having
a second wedding in Las Vegas with Fluffy as the maid
of honor. Then, after she made the woman read it aloud,
Dr. Maude asked her what part exactly made her think
that he was going to leave. After a lot of "Ahhh . . . well . . .
ummm's," the woman had to admit that she didn't have
an answer, and by the end of the show, not only had she
stopped crying, but she was laughing.

When I first suggested to Malia that she make a list of
all the facts about Sam and the way he acted toward her,
she thought it sounded dumb. But after I told her that,
according to Dr. Maude's website, she had a 92 percent
success rate, she agreed.

The Reality List was really handy when a person was
being completely nuts and believing the lies their heads
told them. Like, say, that they were ugly and no one liked
them. It was hard to believe that as pretty as Malia was—
because she was biracial, her skin was the same color as
hot chocolate, and she had long dark hair all the way
to her butt—she would think that, but she did. Which
made her massively shy around boys.

I held out my hand. "Let's see it."

With a sigh she dug it out of her notebook and

handed it to me. "*The Facts Surrounding Me and Sam Meltzer That Might Give People the Impression That He Likes Me Even Though I Know They're Wrong by Malia Powers,*" I read. Beatrice rolled her eyes. "*Number one: He keeps telling all of you, "Not that I like her or anything, but that Malia girl isn't horrible."*"

We all nodded. This was true. Not only that, but he got all red faced when he said it.

"*Two,*" I continued, "*he's always complimenting me on my drawing.*" With two artists for parents, Malia was really good at sketching. Unlike me, who couldn't do more than stick figures. Not only was it her hobby, but she had even won contests for it. I bet Alan would've loved to have had her for a stepdaughter. "*And three: I overheard him say to Max Bellack that if there was a school dance, he'd ask me—*"

Wait a minute—what?! The three of us turned to her. "He *did*?!" we shouted in stereo.

She turned red. "Did I not mention that part?" she mumbled.

I sighed. "Malia, you do realize that this is all just a case of your mind playing tricks on you because that's what a neurotic person's mind does, right?" I asked. That was what Dr. Maude had said to the Fluffy-the-cat woman after she read her list. *Neurotic* was a big word both on Dr. Maude's show and in New York City. Pete was always saying that I was one of the few people in the city who wasn't neurotic. Laurel, on the other hand, with her Purell habit, was. And Alan and his typed agendas for every Official Parker-Moses Family Meeting? He *definitely* was.

She shrugged. "I guess."

"And you understand that your belief that you don't deserve love is an outdated idea that comes from some traumatic event in your childhood, and it's time to put that to rest and move on and seize your destiny, right?" I asked.

"What traumatic event?" she asked.

I shrugged. "I don't know."

"Plus, who said anything about *love*?!"

"Okay, not love," I corrected. "I meant a date for the dance."

"Lucy, what does that whole thing you just said even mean?"

"Um, I'm not entirely sure," I admitted. "But Dr. Maude says it to almost every guest, and every time she does, the audience goes nuts."

She shook her head. "I don't know," she said. "I feel like I really need to look some of those words up on dictionary.com before I say yes or no."

I sighed. "Okay, I'll try this another way. You know how you told us that story a few weeks ago about how, for years, you were scared to try and do a back walkover in gymnastics?"

She nodded. Not only could she draw, but she was good at balancing. I, on the other hand, couldn't even do a cartwheel because of my coordination issues.

"What I want to know is, why would anyone *want* to do a back walkover?" Beatrice asked, taking a bite of her sardine sandwich. Beatrice ate a sardine sandwich every day for lunch. Other than fried clams from Friendly's, I couldn't stand anything fish-like, so the fact that I was BFFs with someone who (a) was a fish lover, and (b) only wore all black while I was so into color was very strange. "I heard about this girl who actually *broke her neck* doing one—"

"Beatrice, you're not helping," I said. I turned back to Malia. "And then without even knowing what you were doing, like you were in a trance or something, you just leaned backward and did it?"

"I saw this TV show once," Alice interrupted, "where this guy named the Amazing Elroy put this woman in a trance—"

"Alice, that sounds fascinating, but I'm in the middle of trying to convince Malia of something," Once more, I turned back to Malia. "And then, after that, you weren't scared ever again?"

A big smile came over her face. "Yeah. And not only that, but it was what won me the silver medal in the mock Olympics at my school in Milan." Malia's dad was Italian, so she had spent the last two years in Italy, which was really cool. Especially because she was fluent in Italian, which meant that the guy at Lombardi's gave us free garlic knots.

"Well, it's kind of like that," I said. "If you never ask

Sam to the dance, you'll never know if he'll say yes. And if he *does* say yes, then from then on, you won't be afraid to ask other boys to dances." I left out the "Although I don't know why anyone would want to ask a boy to a dance anyway" part, because I didn't think it would help the situation. "But even if he says no—which, from what you just told us, doesn't seem like it's going to happen— at least you can be proud of yourself for trying." That part I had stolen from my dad. He was very big on the "be proud of yourself for trying" stuff which, when it came to anything coordination- or math-related or vegan food, was about as far as I got.

She thought about it. "I guess you're right," she admitted. "Okay—I'll ask him."

"You will?!" I asked excitedly.

She shrugged. "I guess."

Beatrice turned to me. "Huh. That was pretty good," she said, impressed.

"Thanks," I replied gratefully. It was hard to impress Beatrice.

"Okay, but what about me?" Alice asked. "I need some advice about Max. Pleeeeeeassse," she moaned, leaning over the lunch table and clutching my arm.

I tried to yank it back, but I couldn't. With her knobby knees and arms that looked a little bit like spaghetti strands, Alice was on the scrawny side, but when it came to anything having to do with Max Rummel? Watch out. It was like the mere mention of his name brought out all this super-human strength in her. Max had been her local crush since second grade. He referred to Alice as "the Stalker." If someone had called me that, I'd be beyond embarrassed, but Alice was proud of it. ("He thinks about me enough to have taken the time to come up with a *nickname* for me!" she squealed when she found out.)

It was either come up with something, or have to walk around with her glued to my side saying "Pleeeeeease . . . pleeeeeease" until I did. I sighed. "Okay, I think in this particular situation, what's needed is some . . . reverse psychology," I said. Dr. Maude was also big on the reverse-psychology stuff.

"What does that mean again?" she asked.

"It means . . . doing something the opposite way that you *want* to do it, or how someone would think you'd do it, but getting the result you want," I replied. At least that's what I thought it meant.

"Ooh, I like that!" Alice gasped. "So what do I do?"

I thought about it. "Okay, you know how Max already knows you like him and that you want to ask him to the dance?"

"You think he knows?" she asked.

Beatrice rolled her eyes. "Alice, people all the way in China who don't speak English know it."

I turned to Beatrice and brushed the hair out of my eyes. To most people, it wouldn't have looked like anything, but because we were BFFs, she knew that it was a Please-don't-be-mean-or-else-this-is-going-to-take-even-longer look. That was the great thing about BFFs—you didn't have to waste a lot of time or energy when you were communicating.

"Okay, okay," she grumbled. "Go on."

I turned back to Alice. "So what you do," I continued, "is, next time you're stalk—I mean, next time you happen to be around him—instead of trying to get his attention like you always do, you . . . ignore him."

She gasped. "*Ignore* Max?"

I nodded. "Yeah. And really loudly you say something like 'The Sadie Hawkins dance is coming up. Too bad there's no one even halfway interesting in this school to ask.'" That part wouldn't be hard for Alice on account of the fact that her whisper was about twenty times louder than most people's outside voices.

"Who do I say that to?" she asked.

I shrugged. "Whoever's with you," I replied.

"But what if I'm alone? Then do I just say it out loud to myself? Will that seem a little weird?" she asked. "Will he think I'm crazy, like I have multiple personalities or something? Because I saw a movie on cable once where a woman had those and—"

I sighed. It was a good thing I was a lot nicer than Dr. Maude, because if Alice was on her show, Dr. Maude would totally yell at her for asking such dumb questions. "Alice, I'm sure you'll figure that part out," I interrupted.

"But the thing of it is, you need him to think that you suddenly changed your mind and you don't like him anymore."

"I *do*?" she asked, confused.

I nodded. "Yeah, 'cause then he'll start getting all worried."

"He *will*?" she asked, even more confused.

"Not to be mean or anything," Beatrice said, "but personally I think he'll probably be really *relieved*."

"See, that's the thing—you'd *think* he would, and he'd probably *say* he would, but the truth is, he's a boy. And boys get freaked out when girls who like them don't like them anymore."

"They do?" asked Malia.

"Well, yeah," I said. "I mean, I don't actually know that from personal experience, but I remember that Madison once did that in an episode with one of her crushes, and it totally worked." Madison—the character Laurel played in her series *The World According to Madison Tennyson*—was even more boy-crazy than Alice. Laurel didn't have a lot of experience with boys. In fact, before Austin Mackenzie (the male equivalent of Laurel in the teen superstar world), who she was kind-of-sort-of-dating in the way that huge stars who live in different cities can date, she had never had a boyfriend.

"Really? Well, if it worked for Madison, it's good enough for me," Alice said. She was a huge Madison fan.

She had every single one of the trading cards *and* the almost-impossible-to-find sleeping bag.

"But that's a TV show," Beatrice said. "And everyone knows that stuff always works out right in a TV show after the character learns a lesson, even if it's at the very last minute."

I turned to Beatrice and scratched the side of my nose, which, in BFF speak, meant, Please be quiet so we can stop talking about this.

"Fine. Okay, so what about me?" Beatrice asked. "What should I do about Chris?"

Chris Linn was Beatrice's local crush. I didn't know him all that well because he was in the drama club, and I tended to stay away from the drama kids because they were always asking me a zillion questions about Laurel and her "process" with her acting. But the few times I had talked to him, he was really nice and funny. If Beatrice and I hadn't been BFFs, I probably would have chosen him as my local crush. Plus, he had a dog named Buster who, from the pictures he had on his Facebook page, looked really cute.

Chris was in Beatrice's tae kwon do class, which was right after school on Thursdays (something Alan had been on me to try before I convinced him that people with coordination issues weren't good at that kind of stuff). Sometimes they ended up riding the subway together. That would be a great time for her to get to know him, if he actually talked to her, but he never did. Instead, she said he focused on the subway ads as if they were *really* interesting, even though I knew from experience that after the first five times you read them, they got boring. Even Dr. Jonathan Zizmor's, who promised that "Now you can have beautiful clear skin!" even if you didn't have the money to pay for it right away.

"Well, you can always—" I started to say.

"So this is what I'm thinking," Beatrice said, cutting me off. "Right before tae kwon do, I'm going to say, 'Chris, you're coming to the Sadie Hawkins dance with me—'"

I loved Beatrice, but she could sometimes be what Mom called a "control freak" (I overlistened to her describing my grandmother one time). "Um, maybe you want to think about—" I started to say.

"And then I'll say, 'And you're going to wear all black,'" she went on, "'so we match. And you're going to have to get a haircut because your hair is too shaggy—'"

"Whoa, Beatrice!" I finally yelled.

"What?"

"Can I give you a piece of advice?"

She shrugged. "I don't know. I guess so. It depends on what it is. What is it?" she asked suspiciously.

Wait a minute. Had she not asked me for advice in the first place? "Have you heard the phrase 'You catch more bees with honey than peanut butter'?" I asked.

"Actually, I think it's 'than with vinegar,'" Malia said.

I thought about it. "Yeah, I think you're right." Malia was a big reader, so she knew these things. Dr. Maude always used that phrase, but most of the time when I watched her show, I ate apples with peanut butter, which is why I think I screwed it up.

"What does *that* mean?" Alice asked.

"It means that if you want someone to do something for you, you're going to have a lot more luck if you're sweet. Not, you know, *ordering them around.*"

"Did you hear that from Dr. Maude?" Beatrice asked.

"Maybe," I lied.

They looked at me.

"Okay. Fine. Yes. Yes, I did. But I would've come up with it on my own," I said. "I mean, it's just plain logic." As someone who didn't understand why clothes had to be put away in drawers when they were just going to be taken out again, I was very good at logic.

"Well, I'll think about it," Beatrice said. "It might work."

I took my advice notebook out from my tote bag so I could add the bees and honey thing in. Now that we had covered all of them and how they were going to get dates for the dance, that just left me, and I did *not* want to go there. Especially since I hadn't yet figured out how I was going to pull off Operation Broken-But-Not-Really Ankle. "So how about the new paint color in the girls' bathroom near the gym?" I asked in an attempt to change the subject. "Would you say it's light blue or lavender?"

Malia turned to me. "What about you, Lucy? Who are you going to ask?"

Great. Just when I had thought I had managed to make it out alive. "To what?" I asked innocently.

"To the *dance*," Beatrice replied.

"Ohh, the *dance*!" I exclaimed. It was a good thing I had no interest in being an actress like Laurel, because from the looks they gave me, I clearly wasn't very good at it. "I don't know." I pointed to my foot. "I twisted my ankle pretty bad this morning, and if it doesn't get better, I might not be able to walk let alone dance, so it's probably better if I just stay home that night."

"But it's still three weeks away," Malia said.

"Yeah, but it was a very twisty twist," I replied.

"But you have to go!" Alice exclaimed. "You're class president."

I dug in my tote bag for the Official By-Laws of the Student Government of the Center for Creative Learning packet that I carried around with me at all times. "Actually, I checked and there's nothing in here that says I do."

Beatrice's eyes narrowed. "Is this because you don't have a local crush to ask?"

"*No*," I replied. It wasn't completely a lie. I actually did have a local crush—I just hadn't gone public with it.

"I bet I could get my cousin Timmy to go with you," Alice offered. "He's got a lazy eye, so it's hard to know where to look when you're talking to him, but, still, he's a boy—"

Luckily for me the bell rang to signal that lunch was over. But this was not good. I may have been able to give my friends good advice, but what was I going to do about *me*?

"Okay, so lemme make sure I got this straight," Pete said later as he sat at his doorman desk in our lobby while I sat on the couch. It was really comfy, and perfect for sprawling, but Pete had told me that because it was a fancy building, the people who lived there looked down on that kind of thing. "Nowadays the girls gotta ask the boys to dances?"

"Well, not always," I replied, pulling down on my hair to make it grow, which was something Alice had read in a magazine. So far, I hadn't noticed a difference, other than the fact that it made my scalp hurt, but I was giving it a try. "But to this one, yeah, because it's a Sadie Hawkins dance."

"Who's Sadie Hawkins?"

"Some cartoon character from the old days," I replied,

trying not to sound impatient. Unlike a lot of adults, Pete paid attention to kids when they talked, which was nice. However, that meant he asked a lot of questions, which tended to make conversations drag on forever.

"Okay. Got it. So you're thinking that if you ask anyone, it's gonna be Blair Lerner-Moskovitz because you recently decided that he's your official local crush even though you haven't told Beatrice yet because you're afraid that she'll think that's a bad choice."

I slid down on the couch. Even though there was no one in the lobby at the moment, did he really have to announce it like that? "Yeah. That pretty much sums it up." I pointed to my foot. "But I hurt my ankle kind of bad this morning, so I don't think I should go because I probably wouldn't be able to dance anyway—"

He shook his head. "Your ankle is fine."

"How do you know?"

"I'm a doorman. We know about these things," he replied. Apparently, doormen knew about everything. "But the answer to this thing is easy."

"It is?"

He nodded. "Sure."

I leaned forward. Although I already had an idea of what he was going to say, I was hoping I was wrong. In fact, I didn't even bother to take out my advice notebook.

"You just have to follow your heart and be yourself," he announced. "And who yourself happens to be is someone who has a crush on Blair Lerner-Moskovitz."

Yup. I was right. More of this "be yourself" stuff. Just hearing Blair's name made me turn red. "Can you just say B.L.M from now on?" I whispered.

"Fine. B.L.M. You have a crush on B.L.M., and you want to ask him to the dance."

I turned even redder. "Do you really have to say the words B.L.M and crush in the same sentence?" I was really not liking this whole crushing-on-a-boy thing—it was so embarrassing!

He sighed. "All I'm gonna say is that if Beatrice is a true friend—and she is—then even if she questions your taste in boys, ultimately she'll respect the fact that because it's a free country, you can like whoever you want."

I sighed. "Okay, okay."

"Because if you're not yourself, and you're not honest about your feelings, it always ends up biting you in the butt," he added.

I sighed again. "I know." I had learned that a bunch of times in the last year, especially when it came to Laurel, Dad, and Mom. As scared as I had been to do it, I had had some really honest conversations with them about stuff—like how I was feeling ignored—and in each case things ended up working out. Not only that, but talking about stuff made whatever stomach pains I was having go away. Actually, the more I thought about it, maybe I should talk to Alan about this whole hobby and college thing, too.

"So are you going to do it?" Pete asked.

"Maybe," I said.

Which was better than "absolutely positively not."

chapter 2

Dear Dr. Maude,

This is going to have to be short because instead of studying for my algebra test, I just spent the last two hours watching *Surf Safari* on cable. Connor Forrester's in it. He and I have become really good friends through our Triple S's (Skype Snack Sessions). I had to watch out of loyalty, even though I'd already seen it five times. I wish I didn't find him so goofy because he'd be the perfect celebrity crush for me—especially since we ended up kissing in the parking lot of In-N-Out Burger that time I was out in L.A. with Laurel. But I don't *like* him like-him. He's just not my type. He's too . . . movie star-ish. Which would make sense, seeing that he is a movie star. And also he's what my dad would call "not the sharpest tool in the shed."

I'm not exactly sure what my type is, but I think it's more of someone like Blair. You know, a little messy. Cute but not super-cute. Someone who likes interesting snack foods such as fried Oreos.

But before I go study, I needed to let you know that I'm not going to be able to write to you anymore. It's not because

I finally realized that me being your most loyal fan ever means nothing to you and you're never going to write me back. And it's not that when I stop to think about it, you show 7 of the Top 10 Warning Signs That Someone Is Not a Good Friend thing that you have on your website.

Nope—the real reason is . . . well, actually, I can't tell you the reason because it's a huge secret, and even though you probably wouldn't tell anyone because that would mean first READING MY E-MAIL, Beatrice thinks it's smart if I don't tell anyone outside of my immediate family about this. (When I say "this," I mean the thing I don't feel comfortable telling you about.) Just so you know, it's not like what I'm doing is illegal or anything like that. In fact, if it works out, I'll be helping a ton of people. They just won't actually know I'm helping them because of the whole secret part of it all.

So I just wanted to say that it's been nice writing to you. The funny thing is that I sure could use some advice about this thing I can't tell you about. Oh well. I guess I'll just have to come up with some myself.

Oh—but if you wanted to give me advice about the thing with Alan and how he's disappointed in me as a daughter because I don't have any hobbies and will therefore not be going to college, I think that would be okay. You know, seeing that all that happened before this new thing. Especially because I'm having trouble getting advice from anyone else.

Well, thanks for everything. I'm not sure what the

"everything" is, seeing that you never actually did anything, but it sounds like the kind of thing you say to someone in a final e-mail.

yours truly,
Lucy B. Parker

P.S. Just in case you're worried that I might go ask Dr. Dave for advice on this secret issue, I'm not going to.

I guess I could've talked to Mom about the Alan stuff, but I was afraid she'd get all freaked out and insist on an EPMFM (Emergency Parker-Moses Family Meeting) and tell Alan how I was feeling, right in front of me. And talking to Laurel about it wouldn't work because she'd (a) say it wasn't true, and then (b) run and tell him in hopes of helping but, really, would just make it worse.

There was Dad, but asking your dad for advice about your other dad felt weird, too. What if he got all mad at Alan? Or jealous that I cared so much about what Alan thought? Now that I had two families, I understood why some of my friends with blended families had stomach problems. Having to worry about the feelings of not just one family, but two (or in the case of Haley Jenkins, whose parents had each been remarried, three) dealing with so many people was stressful.

Which is why I decided the only person I could trust with this particular issue was Ziggy. At only a month old he couldn't respond with words yet, but I knew him well enough to be able to know what his various squawks and mewls meant.

When I texted Dad and Sarah to say that I needed an emergency Skype session with Ziggy, even though it was right before his nap time, they weren't thrilled. Which I didn't understand since Sarah, as a yoga person, was always going on about how we should all just go with the flow and let the Universe do its thing. Plus, because he was a baby, he slept a lot, so I didn't think it was that big of a deal if I borrowed him for fifteen minutes.

After I begged a little more and said how it would go a long way in helping me bond with him, they said yes. When Dad connected us and I appeared on the screen and started yelling, "Hi Ziggy! Look over here! It's Lucy! Your sister!" I swear that not only did he smile but the noise that came out of his mouth sounded very much like "Hiiii." After Dad shot some video of Ziggy and me talking (I made him swear not to post it on Facebook because of a zittage issue on my part), I asked him if he could please give us some alone time. From the look on Dad's face I could see that he was disappointed.

But because, like Alan, he was big on everyone having individual bonding time, he agreed.

"Hey, Ziggy, how are you?" I yelled when we were alone. Dad said it wasn't necessary for me to do that—that an inside voice was just fine—but between the Skype thing, and the fact that Ziggy's ears were the size of small apple slices, I didn't want to risk him not hearing what I was saying. I knew him well enough to know that the "Ahhhh" that came out of his tiny mouth was Babyese for "Other than the fact that my mom's being annoying because she wants to put this sticky, gunky essential oil on me that's supposed to prevent teething pain even though I'm nowhere near that yet, I'm fine."

"I'm glad to hear it," I yelled. "So listen—I know that because you've only been alive for forty-two days, you don't have a ton of life experience, but I was wondering if I could run something by you."

It would have been obvious to anyone who had ever passed a hearing test that his "Ghhheeee" definitely meant "Sure. Because you're such an awesome older sister, I'd be happy to help you out any way I can."

"Great. Thanks. So here's the deal—" I yelled.

"Lucy, inside voice, please," I heard Dad yell from outside the door.

"Dad! You're overlistening!" I yelled. "This is *private*—between me and Ziggy!" I had to admit, if anyone had told me just two months before that I'd actually *want* to talk to my baby brother and think his name was cute rather than embarrassing, I would've thought they were nuts.

I was ashamed to admit it now, but back when Dad had told me that he and Sarah were pregnant, I wasn't very excited. In fact, I was very worried that he'd become Dad's favorite kid and I'd be left behind. But like Dad had said, when your family gets bigger, your heart has this way of stretching to make room for all the new people in your life. Kind of like my old teacher Mrs. Kline's elastic-waist pants.

"Okay, okay, I'm going," Dad said.

I waited a moment. "I can still hear you breathing!" I yelled. Actually, I couldn't, but that was how Mom busted me all the time so I figured I'd give it a try.

"Like I said, I'm going." This time I heard him walk away.

If he were still overlistening, Dad would've said it was a gas bubble, but I swear Ziggy was laughing. I leaned in closer to the screen. "Okay. That's better. So here's the deal, Zig. I was thinking that because you were born into a family where your dad is a Buddhist and believes in reincarnation, because you're the most recently reincarnated out of all of us, you probably have the most life experience and therefore you're the smartest."

He made a *pfffft*-sounding sound, which I took to mean, "You got that right."

I nodded. "That's what I thought. Okay, so this is my problem—"

The *eee-ohh* that came out of his little mouth

definitely meant "You do? But you don't deserve to have any problems. You're my super-cool older sister!"

I shrugged. "I know. I agree that it's not fair, but what are you going to do. So the problem is this." I took a deep breath and told him everything. About the hobby issues. About the fact that even though Alan was nice to me, I still felt like I was disappointing him. And, of course, about the Sadie Hawkins dance. I hadn't realized how much I needed to get off my chest.

Even though Ziggy didn't say anything, just knowing he was listening made me feel better. Plus, because he couldn't talk, he couldn't say annoying things like "Oh Lucy—don't you think you're overreacting?"

"So what do you think, Zig?" I asked after I had spewed everything and caught my breath. "Any advice on how I should handle this?"

Unfortunately, all I got in response was tiny little baby snores that sounded a little like Miss Piggy's.

"Ziggy? Are you sleeping?"

More snores.

"Oh," I said, disappointed. I wish I had known at exactly what point he had fallen asleep, but it wasn't like he could tell me. I leaned in closer. "Are you SURE you're sleeping?" I yelled.

This time he responded with a little fart.

I sighed. "Okay. Well, thanks for listening. To however much you heard before you conked out."

So much for *that* plan.

Laurel was actually the one who came up with the solution to the hobby issue the next day. It was the day of the Plagiarizing Incident. According to Beatrice, the Plagiarizing Incident was the most drama that had happened at the Center since anyone could remember.

I had to say, it was nice that, finally, there was an Incident-with-a-capital-I that didn't have to do with me. After the Straightening Iron Incident (where I burned off one of my pigtails because I had thought leaving it on for a half hour was a good idea), the Hat Incident (the first time I met Laurel, when the director of her movie took my hat off my head, exposing my super-short haircut, which made me look like an egghead), the Poster Incident (when Cristina Pollock put up very unflattering pictures of me during the election), I had had enough Incidents to last me for my entire life.

I knew from a vocab test the year before that plagiarism meant "the unauthorized use or close imitation of the language and thoughts of another author and the representation of them as one's own work," but I had never known anyone who had actually ever committed it. It was one thing to give a report and say, "According to the *World Encyclopedia* . . ." and then go on and read three pages from it, which is what Alex Campbell did during his report on Zimbabwe last year. But to pass off stuff as your own? And then when people say, "Wow—this is really great. You're so talented!" and you just sit there and are all "Aww, gee, thanks"? That's just *wrong*.

If the person who had been caught plagiarizing was someone like Martin Van Oy (he was one of those kids with what Alan called "behavioral problems," which, for some reason, he always said in a whisper, like he did when he mentioned the word *cancer*) or Nick Costas (another nonsharp tool in the shed), that would've been one thing. But the fact that it was Susan Milken was a total scandal.

Susan was one of those kids who, if you couldn't get close enough to hear her breathing and smell her tuna-fish breath, you'd swear she was a robot. Not only did she always raise her hand in class and wait to be called on, but she never ran in the halls, not even on Taco Tuesdays, which was the best lunch of the week. And, when it came to being organized, she was almost as bad as Laurel. Different-colored folders for each subject, with color-coordinated notebooks, pens, *and* pencils. She was also the girl who wrote the advice column for the *Center for Creative Learning News*, which was the very *un*creative name of our school newspaper (as class president, I was trying to get that changed).

Obviously, I knew what good advice sounded like from all my Dr. Maude watching, and Susan's was *not* good. According to Beatrice, it was very *bourgeois*. Not only did a lot of Susan's responses make no sense in terms of the question being asked—stuff in the vein of "Don't go counting your chickens before they hatch" (We lived in New York City. Not a lot of chickens being grown)—but for a while she was on a rhyming kick. ("Like a tree, you will see, what will be, when you say 'Hey—this is me!'")

After people complained about the rhyming thing, a weird thing happened. Instead of boring questions like "Dear Susan: My piano teacher lives in Tribeca, near the Franklin Street stop. But I live all the way up on 88th and Riverside. So when going down there, is it better to just get on the 1 train at 86th St. and hope that I get a seat so I don't have to stand the whole time because it's a long trip? Or do I get on the 1 and take it to 72nd and switch to the 2 or 3 and take it to 14th and then switch BACK to the 1 to go to Franklin?" suddenly the questions got really good. Like "Dear Susan: I'm totally freaking out because this morning when I woke up, I realized that my BFF and I have completely grown apart, and without even knowing it I've become BFFs with someone else, but I don't know how to tell my old BFF that she's no longer my BFF without hurting her feelings. Help!"

And instead of some dumb answer like "The early bird always catches the worm" Susan answered it with a snappy, funny response, like the ones in the advice columns in Laurel's favorite magazines were written.

Which, thanks to Maysun Rogaway, we now knew was because they *were* the questions and answers from the magazine advice columns!

The day before when Maysun was home sick with the flu, she came across this site called AlbertaAdolescents.com. While the site itself was pretty boring—with articles like "How to Prevent Frostbite" (apparently Alberta, which is in Canada, gets very cold)—when she clicked around she discovered the Advice by Amelia section. The whole time she was reading it, she kept feeling like she had seen the questions and answers. Later on in the day, after watching a few movies on cable and making her dog stay still when she put sunglasses on her so she could take some pictures and upload them on Facebook, the question/answer thing was still bothering her. Which was why she said she took the elevator all the way down to the basement of her building to where the recyclables were to find the most recent copy of the *Center for Creative Learning News*. Thankfully, because she had just thrown it out the night before, it was not only still there but nothing gross had spilled on it. And that was how she was able to find out Susan had just cut and pasted Amelia's questions and answers and used them in her column. Like not-even-bothering-to-change-a-single-word cut and paste.

Because this was such huge news, it wasn't like Maysun could wait until she was back at school the next day to tell people what happened. Which is why she texted her BFF Lilly to tell her the news. And even though we're not supposed to use our electronic devices during school hours (a rule that, of course, Susan always followed), Lilly was always going to the girls' room with hers.

By lunch, everyone in the whole school had heard about the Plagiarizing Incident, including Dr. Rem-Wall. So no one was surprised when, right after lunch, our teacher Mr. Eglington (aka Mr. Eagle Eye) announced that Susan was to report to the office immediately. When she came back to class a half hour later, with her eyes so puffy they were just slits, and picked up her color-coded stuff and left the room again, it was obvious she was in big trouble.

It was such a big scandal that Dr. Rem-Wall ended up calling an emergency school-wide assembly to talk about plagiarism and morals and integrity, which was a little boring, although the fact that I had my Cookie Dough Lip Smacker with me helped. Plus, we got to miss algebra, which was just fine with me.

"Wait a minute—I have the best idea!" Laurel exclaimed as we walked around Central Park after school as part of her workout. She was up for this movie based on a true story about an Olympic skier from Germany who ended up bashing into a tree and going blind. But because most Olympic skiers weren't the string beans Laurel was, she had asked me to be her trainer. Which, luckily, just meant walking with her. Because she was my frister and I loved her, I of course agreed to do it. Only after she offered to pay

49

me ten bucks a walk, which, as far as I was concerned, was a real bargain (seeing that I once heard Mom say to Alan when I was overlistening that the hundred dollars an hour Laurel's real trainer charged was "highway robbery").

"What is it?" I asked warily. A lot of the time her ideas were much better suited for a TV episode than real life.

"*You* should take over the advice column!" she said.

Like, say, that one. "What?!"

"You said everyone was really impressed with the advice you gave them at lunch the other day about the dance," she replied.

"That's because they're my *friends*," I said. "It's easy to give advice to people you love. 'Cause even if it backfires, they can't get *that* mad at you."

"So? As you're coming up with advice, you can just pretend the person you're writing to is your friend."

I gave her a doubtful look. "Like how I was supposed to pretend everyone was in their underwear when I was giving my speech during the election? All that did was gross me out."

"Come on, Lucy—between everything you've learned from Dr. Maude, and your advice notebook, you'd be great at it!" she cried as she gracefully dodged a guy on a bike. I, however, being *un*graceful, ended up twisting my ankle a little. For real this time. Although it hurt, it *would* help me in my I-can't-go-to-the-dance argument.

Laurel pointed at my tote bag, which, in addition to maxi- and minipads, and the crush and period logs, held my advice notebook. "I bet out of the first five pages alone, you'd have enough advice for an entire month's worth of columns!"

"I don't know," I said, doubtfully. "I don't think a class president is able to have that position. It's sort of like a whatdoyoucallit."

"Conflict of interest?" she asked. She reached into her bag and took out her copy of the official by-laws. Laurel didn't even go to my school, but because of her official presidential frister status and her love of order, she kept a copy of the by-laws on her at all times so she could help out whenever she could. She skimmed the pages and shook her head. "Nope. It doesn't say anything in here about the president not being allowed to work on the school paper."

I sighed. Sometimes I hated the fact that she was so organized. "Well, even so, it would be weird. I wouldn't want people thinking they had to take my advice just because I'm president," I said, hobbling to keep up with her.

Laurel stopped walking and turned to me. "Then the class president doesn't have to do it. You could write the column under a *pseudonym*."

Huh. That could be interesting. A pseudonym was a fake name you used when you were trying to hide your identity, like how Laurel used the name Jane Austen at hotels so there weren't ten million fans camped out in the lobby waiting for her. Coming up with the fake name would be almost as fun as writing the column. But still. "I really appreciate your confidence in me," I said. "A lot. But the truth is . . ." I shook my head. "Forget it."

"What is it?"

I felt my face turn red. "Nothing. It's dumb." I hated when people said that to me, but it *was* dumb, and I didn't want to talk about it. I started walking again, but Laurel wasn't following. And I knew she wouldn't until I told her. She hated when people said that, too. "Okay, fine. The truth is, Cristina Pollock wants the job, so that would be one more reason for her to hate me." It felt stupid to still be scared of her, but I was. From my very first lunch in the cafeteria when I mistakenly sat at "her" table and had to be rescued by Beatrice, things between Cristina and me had gone from bad to worse, especially once I beat her in the election.

We started walking again. "Okay, now if someone came to you with that problem, what would you do?" Laurel asked.

"What do you mean?"

"I mean, if you were an advice columnist and someone wrote you that there was something they wanted to do, but they were afraid to do it because the class bully might get mad, what would you tell them?"

I shrugged. "That's easy. One word: *WWYDIYWA*?" That stood for What Would You Do If You Weren't Afraid, which was something I had picked up from Pete. It was so good I had typed it out in twenty-four-point font on a piece of paper and hung it next to my mirror so I wouldn't forget it as I started my day. Laurel had even laminated a copy for me to keep in my locker. Next to her label maker, her laminating machine was her favorite organizational tool.

"That's brilliant!" Laurel cried.

I smiled. I had to admit—it kind of *was*.

"So why don't you take your own advice?"

The smile left my face. It wasn't *that* brilliant.

"I mean, you're so good at giving advice, it's almost like . . . a hobby or something."

Now I was the one who stopped walking. Maybe if I got the job, Alan would be impressed. My own column in the school paper? Not only would that mean I was an expert at something, but it would be a cool thing to put on my applications for college.

If Laurel's idea worked, I wouldn't have to worry about the hobby issue anymore.

"This is starting to feel very homework-like," I said later as we sat in Laurel's very clean room. "It's not like I can just come up with this stuff on the spot, you know. It's an *art*. Like photography." Dad was a photographer, so he was always saying things like that. Especially when money was tight and he was forced to take pet portraits, and the owners got all frustrated when he took so long to do it. "Or origami," I added.

53

She rolled her eyes as Miss Piggy settled in her lap and started purring. I really needed to step up my efforts on Operation New Kitten. If I was ever able to convince Mom and Alan to get me a new kitten, I was going to train it right away to like me best, because having to watch Miss Piggy choose Laurel over me hurt my feelings. "If you get this gig, it's not going to be your *art*," she said. "It's going to be your *job*. So you need to practice." She scribbled something on a piece of paper (although Laurel's "scribbling" was still neater than most people's best handwriting) and handed it to me. "Here—start with this."

"'*Dear Annie*,'" I read aloud. I looked at her. "Who's Annie?" I asked, confused.

"I thought your pseudonym could be Annie the Advice Giver," she replied.

"But I wanted to come up with the name," I said, disappointed. "That's one of the reasons I'm going through with this. I was thinking maybe I could call myself . . . Holly. As in 'Help from Holly.'"

She wrinkled her nose. "Mmm . . . I think you should stick with 'advice' in the title. Otherwise, kids might start asking you for homework help."

Oh, that would NOT be good. I barely had enough time to get my own homework done.

"And we can have a little avatar drawn up," Laurel went on. "Maybe even have someone animate it. You know, like if there ends up being a website. Speaking of which—"

"Whoa, whoa—" I said, interrupting her. Websites? Animation? What had I gotten myself into? "Don't you think we should wait and see if I get the *job* first?"

"I guess you're right," she agreed. Her iPhone buzzed with a text. She smiled. "Austin thinks it's great that you're going to be the new advice columnist."

"Can we *please* slow down here?!" I cried. "I can't have the whole world knowing before I even get the job." Austin tweeted almost as much as my friend Marissa. But unlike her, he had almost a million followers, while Marissa had eleven.

"Okay, okay."

"*'Recently my BFF called me up and said that she no longer wants to be friends with me,'*" I continued reading, "*'but that she still wants to be my plus one to the MTV Movie Awards so she'd like the non-BFF thing to not take effect until after that. What should I do? Signed, BFF-less on Broadway.'*" I looked at her. "Okay, the *idea* of this is really good, but I think we should change the MTV Movie Awards thing to ... 'birthday party,'" I said. "So it's a little more relatable to normal kids."

She nodded. "Good point," she said. Some people may have thought that Laurel was being stuck-up by thinking like this, but it wasn't her fault that she had been famous since she was nine and these things were just part of her daily life.

After I took out a piece of notebook paper and a pencil (if I did end up doing this, that was going to mean

I would need to keep yet another notebook), I slathered some Chocolate Mousse Lip Smacker on my lips. The chocolate really helped me think. I was so making Laurel buy me more Lip Smackers if I got this job.

"Dear BFF-less," I said as I wrote. "Okay, the fact that your *ex*-BFF is so clueless that she'd try to get an invite to your birthday party tells you everything you need to know. It's time to be your OWN BFF and surround yourself with people who don't take you for granted! Good luck, Lucy B. Parker." I stopped and erased the last part. "I mean 'Good luck, *Annie*.'"

"I can't believe you came up with that so fast!" Laurel exclaimed. "The 'time to be your own BFF'? Completely genius!"

I smiled. "Thanks."

She handed me another question. "Try this one."

"'*Dear Annie,*'" I read, "'*This is a little embarrassing to admit, but I'm pretty sure I have a crush on my best friend's brother. But I'm afraid to tell her because she thinks he's an idiot, and I don't want her to think I'm a loser for liking him. How do I handle this? Signed, Worried on West End Ave.*'" My eyes narrowed. "Is this supposed to be about me and Blair?" I demanded. Laurel and Pete were the only ones who knew about my crush.

"*No,*" she said, twisting a lock of hair around her finger.

My eyes narrowed more. "Laurel. You're doing the hair-twisting thing," I said. "Which means you're lying."

Fristers knew these things about each other. Like how Laurel knew that when I played with my left ear, chances were *I* was lying.

"Lucy, you're not the only person in the world who's ever had a crush on her best friend's brother," she scoffed. "I bet there are millions of girls out there in the world who can relate to this. So just answer it."

"*Fine*," I said. "'*Dear Worried*,'" I wrote. "'*Look at it this way: if your favorite ice cream flavor was rainbow sherbet (even though, technically, it's not really ice cream), and your friends made fun of you for it because of how boring a flavor it is, would you give it up as your favorite flavor? No. You'd say something like 'A person can't help what kind of ice cream they like, so let's just move on,' right? Well, it's the same with people—a person can't help who they like. Which is why, when you finally get up the guts to tell your BFF about your crush—NOT THAT YOU HAVE TO RIGHT THIS MINUTE—but when you do, if she gives you any trouble, you should tell her that you don't give her grief for her choice in ice cream. Even though, as far as you're concerned, if she's going to go with chocolate chip, it could at least be mint chocolate chip. Stay true to sherbet, Annie.*'" I looked up at Laurel. "How's that?"

"You did it again!"

I smiled. So what if my sero-whatsitcalled level was lower because I watched TV. All that time spent watching

Dr. Maude was going to help me make a difference in people's lives. *And* get Alan to be proud of me.

When I went down to Beatrice's apartment to show her the fake letters and responses, she was so excited she did a little jig.

"Wait a minute—are you doing a *jig*?" I asked.

She looked over at herself in her bedroom mirror. "I guess I am," she said, before she quickly stopped. Anyone who knew Beatrice knew that she was very anti-jig. She was also anti-skipping and anti-jumping-up-and-down. Pete said that it was part of the whole "jaded New Yorker" thing.

Jaded was when you were too cool to show any excitement about anything, like the fact that two cabbies had gotten out of their taxis in the middle of Times Square during rush hour to start screaming at each other. Beatrice was so jaded that the only way you could tell if she was really excited was if she said "I'm really excited," and even then, it never really sounded all that excited.

She jigged a bit more. "It's just that this is possibly one of the most incredible ideas of all time!" She stopped and flipped through the questions and answers. "You came up with these answers yourself, right? They're not from some advice column from a magazine out of Australia or something?"

"Of course I did!" I replied, offended. "What kind of person do you think I am?"

"Okay, okay—don't get all upset," she said as she flopped down on her very uncomfortable black leather chair. Not only did Beatrice and her family wear all black, but their furniture was mostly black as well, even in their bedrooms *(ew)*. And uncomfortable. "I'm just double-checking." She held up one of the pieces of notebook paper. "This one about the ice cream flavor is *really* good. I bet a lot of people will relate to it. I mean, *I* don't, because no one would ever have a crush on my brother, but people with normal brothers will get it."

I could feel myself start to sweat.

"Not to mention that there's nothing wrong with plain old chocolate chip ice cream," she went on. "In fact, that happens to be my favorite."

Uh-oh. Was Beatrice about to figure out that I had a crush on Blair? I mean, she was pretty smart—especially when it came to word problems, which is kind of what this was. Or was this a sign that I should just come clean and tell her?

Although there wasn't an official BFF handbook (Beatrice and I had been thinking of writing one because we thought we'd be able to make a lot of money off it. Especially if we got Laurel to write the introduction and blog and tweet about it), I'm pretty sure that "No secrets" would be in the top three of the Top Ten Commandments of BFFdom. If someone had written me—or, rather, Annie—a letter saying her guilt over keeping a secret from her BFF was keeping her up at night to the point where sometimes she had to get out of bed and sneak into the kitchen for a snack, I would've told her to just come clean and tell her the truth. And if I was going to become the Center's newest advice columnist, I should probably take my own advice. Otherwise, I'd be a hypocrite. And being a hypocrite was almost as bad as plagiarizing. At least in my book.

I visualized the WWYDIYWA sign next to my mirror. But what *would* I do if I wasn't afraid?

I'd tell her. And then I'd run out the door to the elevator as fast as I could.

I took a deep breath. "Beatrice, there's something I have to tell you," I said nervously.

She stopped trying to make her stick-straight black bob curly and looked over at me. "What is it?"

I looked down at my left armpit. *Ew.* I was sweating so much there was already a little bit of a stain. "Well, see, the thing is . . . I . . ." I took another deep breath. I could do this. And once I did, I'd feel so much better. Unless I died of embarrassment before the feeling-better part. "I've been doing a lot of thinking about this lately, and what I need you to know is . . ."

Beatrice was looking at me like I was nuts. Probably because I *was* nuts. I took a deep breath. ". . . that I feel really bad that I haven't been more understanding and respectful of your choice to choose whatever ice cream flavor you want," I continued. "And I don't think there's anything wrong with chocolate chip being a person's favorite flavor."

Apparently, I couldn't do this. That was okay. Was being afraid really *that* bad? Lots of people got afraid. Like Laurel, when she had to have lunch with the First Family at the White House. Although that wasn't a great example, because that's definitely a time to be afraid. I mean, what if you mistakenly pushed some button that blew up the world or something?

She smiled. "Thanks. I really appreciate that. Especially because I know how seriously you take the subject of ice cream."

"You're welcome." Could I save this? "I know I tease you about how boring it is, and, sure, I tend to go for the more interesting flavors like Chunky Monkey and Blueberries and Cream, but it's totally a free country." Apparently, I could not. Not only could I not tell her about my crush, but now I had to start bloversharing to boot.

"And I'm sorry that I'm always saying what a disgusting and *bourgeois* combination Canadian bacon and pineapple is on pizza," Beatrice said. "Because even though you couldn't pay me a million dollars to eat it myself, like you said, it's a free country."

I stopped myself from saying that, actually, it was quite delicious—especially the way they made it at V&T's, on account of the fact that they always got the amounts just right, unlike Two Boots, where they tended to put on too much ham and not enough pineapple. "Thanks. I really appreciate that, too," I replied.

She came over and hugged me. "It's so great that we can be so honest with each other," she said.

At least one of us can, I thought to myself as I patted her on the back.

"And I think you're going to make an awesome advice columnist," she said.

I sure hoped so. Because I definitely wasn't an awesome truth teller.

chapter 3

Dear Dr. Maude,

I know I said that I wasn't going to write to you anymore, but I just wanted to check and make sure that I didn't hurt your feelings by telling you that. Seriously, it is SO not personal. In fact, it's got nothing to do with you. Because, you know, not everything in the world does, Dr. Maude. (Mom always says that to me when I get all sensitive.)

Anyway, I wish I could tell you what's going on, because if I did, then you'd see that I'm telling the truth. But like I said in my last e-mail, I just can't. But if you didn't READ my last e-mail—which you probably DIDN'T—that won't make any sense.

I also wanted to tell you that I really miss our friendship. I know it was just me writing to you and you never responding, so it wasn't really a regular friendship, like the ones where people share equally, but still, it felt like one. Well, at least on the days that my feelings weren't hurt because you hadn't written me back. Which, now that we're no longer in touch, I can tell you were A LOT.

Anyway, that's all I wanted to say. And now you REALLY won't be hearing from me again.

yours truly,
Lucy B. Parker

P.S. Also—I hope you're not worrying about the Dr. Dave stuff, either. Because there's no reason to. I swear. But I totally understand if you are, because I get all paranoid about that kind of stuff, too.

Maybe I was a wuss when it came to coming clean to my best friend about the fact that even if she thought her brother could be kind of annoying at times, he was the least annoying of all the boys I knew. But it didn't mean I couldn't be brave in *other* areas of my life—like, say, raising my hand in homeroom when Mr. Eagle Eye asked during announcements if anyone was interested in taking over the advice column.

Except, unfortunately, I was a wuss *then*, too.

"No one other than Cristina is interested? Really?" he asked. I pulled my purple corduroy beret down so it almost covered my eyes. "That's too bad. You know, when I was your age—" The entire class sighed.

Mr. Eagle Eye was very big on telling us stories about what it was like to grow up in the old days before e-mail and texting.

"Then I guess it's all mine," Cristina announced smugly as she flipped her long blonde hair. It really wasn't fair that someone so mean had such nice hair. Or such small boobs.

Mr. Eagle Eye was halfway through rolling his eyes before he remembered he was a teacher and shouldn't do those sorts of things because it set a bad example. (The reason I knew that was what he was thinking was because once, when the door to the teachers' lounge was open, I happened to hear him say that to Mrs. Collett.)

Beatrice snapped one of my rainbow suspenders from behind. Lucky for us, Mr. Eagle Eye didn't make us sit in alphabetical order.

"Ow!" I cried.

"Tell him," she hissed.

"Tell him what?" I hissed back.

"About Annie!"

He looked over at us. "Girls, do you have something you'd like to share with the class?"

I never understood why teachers said that. Didn't they realize that if it was something I wanted to share, I'd raise my hand and say "Excuse me? Mr. Eagle—I mean, Mr. Eglington? There's something I'd like to share with the class," instead of whispering behind his back?

"No," I replied

"Yes," Beatrice said.

I gave her a look.

"Lucy knows someone who's interested in the position," she announced.

"Super! Who's that, Lucy?" he asked. Everything with Mr. Eagle Eye was "super" or "wonderful."

"Uh, well, her name is Annie," I replied. I looked down at my right armpit. Great. More sweating.

"Annie Miller?" he asked. Annie Miller was the captain of the girls' basketball team. Because I tended to stay away from all things sports-related, I didn't know her well, but from the few conversations I had had with her, back when I was campaigning for president, it seemed like pretty much the only thing she would've been able to give advice on was basketball and where to find size-twelve sneakers.

"Actually, it's not *really* Annie . . . it's something else," I babbled. "That's her whatchamacallit—her—"

"It's her pseudonym," Beatrice said.

"What a wonderful word choice, Beatrice!" Mr. Eagle Eye said. "I'm very impressed. Class, if you recall, pseudonym was one of our recent vocabulary words. Can anyone tell me what it means?" Other than the *whoosh* of Petra Sampson's hand (three-time spelling bee champion and all-around butt kisser) going up in the air, the room was silent. "Okay, well then, moving on. So you were saying, Lucy?"

"She's using a pseudonym because she wants to remain anonymous. So, you know, there aren't any death threats against her in case people don't like the advice," I babbled. It totally wasn't fair that I outgrew my bras every few months, but I couldn't outgrow my bloversharing habit. Now my left armpit was sweating. "Because, you know, sometimes when people hear things they don't want to hear, they get upset," I went on. "But she goes to the school."

"Wait a minute—I know nothing about this! How come you guys didn't tell me about this Annie person?" Alice demanded, all hurt.

I turned to her. "We were going to. At lunch," I replied. Telling Alice anything was like posting it on Facebook, tweeting it, *and* having it on the front page of the *New York Post*, which is why I had wanted to hold off as long as possible.

"Excuse me, but this is illegal!" Cristina cried. "An anonymous person can't have the position. It's in the by-laws."

"Oh no, it's not," Beatrice said with a smirk. "I already checked." Even though it had been a year since Cristina had friend-dumped her, Beatrice still held a huge grudge against her. Which, having been friend-dumped myself by these two girls Rachel and Missy right before sixth grade started, I totally understood, even if Dad was always going on about how grudges weren't good for your karma.

"Well, it should be," Cristina said. She stood up and planted her hands on her hips. "I'm telling my father about this. We'll sue if we have to."

Mr. Eagle Eye couldn't hide the eye roll then. Not that you could blame the guy. Cristina was *always* saying, "We'll sue if we have to!" That was because her dad was a big lawyer. With ads on the subway and everything. Although once when I was overlistening, I heard Alan tell Mom that anyone whose face was plastered on public transportation gave lawyers like himself (he gave up his job as one to manage Laurel when she got successful) a bad name. "Cristina, we'll let Dr. Remington-Wallace decide this, okay?"

"Fine. But I'm telling you right now—that job is *mine*," she sniffed.

I looked down at my desk. With the way my stomach already felt like there were Mexican jumping beans in it, I was tempted to just give it to her.

What would I do if I weren't afraid?

The answer to that didn't really matter because I *was* afraid.

Since there was more than one person who wanted the job, the Advice Column Committee had Cristina and I—I mean "Annie"—come up with some sample answers. The Center was very big on committees, so no one was surprised when one had been put together to pick the new advice columnist. Although what Mr. Perez, the gym teacher, knew about any sort of advice giving that didn't have to do with volleyball or basketball was a mystery to me.

Between worrying about how to get out of going to the dance (unfortunately, my twisted ankle had already healed) and waiting for the Advice Column Committee to review the sample answers and choose the winner, I had enough on my plate. So when Alan came into my room the next evening to tell me that we had to move our IBS to that weekend, it was just one more thing for me to stress about.

"You know how I feel about the importance of routine and not rearranging things, Lucy," he said as I tried to spread my homework out to make it look like I was studying rather than watching *America's Top Puppy* on Animal Planet. "But this meeting of the Upper West Siders Backgammon Club is going to be an important one. Claude Warner's been gunning for the presidency for a year now, and if that happens, the fate of the club as we know it is doomed."

Before moving to New York I had had no idea what backgammon was, but once I moved in with Alan, I couldn't escape it. It was this weird game that was a little like checkers, but not really, played with little round pieces made of stone. He had tried to explain it to me many times (one whole IBS was spent on the game), but as patient as he was, I couldn't get it. All I knew was it had to do with rolling some dice and then moving the pieces across the board trying to get them "home." Or, in my case, trying not to drop them so they rolled underneath couches and were lost forever.

"Oh yeah. You've mentioned him before," I said. "You know if you want to hold off on our IBS until next month—"

"Of course not," he replied. "We'll just do it this weekend. That is, if you're free."

"I'm . . ." Was I going to lie? It's not like I could afford bad karma at the moment. ". . . free on Sunday. But I think we're having an algebra test on Monday, so I was hoping to spend the day studying." So maybe that part was a teensy tiny little bit of a lie.

"Oh. Well, I certainly don't want to take you away from that," Alan said. "But when we do reschedule it, I was thinking we could walk over to the Ninety-second Street Y and check out what classes they're offering for teens. I think I remember seeing a lifeguarding prep course that looked interesting—"

Lifeguarding? With my coordination, I'd definitely kill someone. "Well, the thing is . . . I think I may have found a hobby already."

"You did?! What is it?" Alan asked excitedly. "Did

you give the clogging class some more thought?" Clogging was this weird dance style where you stomped your feet a lot. "Like I keep saying, colleges are always looking for students who aren't afraid to follow the beat of their own drummer—ooh—wait a minute. What about *drumming*? That could be interesting. I think I saw a flyer about an African drumming class at Whole Foods. Obviously, you couldn't practice in the apartment—"

"It's nothing music- or dance-related," I interrupted. "It's ... advice giving."

"What?"

"I'm auditioning to become the new advice columnist in the school newspaper," I explained.

Alan did that thing where he closed his left eye and wrinkled his nose, which meant he was thinking extra hard. I really hoped he liked the idea of me being an advice columnist, because I was getting tired just thinking about the idea of coming up with more ideas, or worse, letting him come up with more ideas. Although the idea of African drumming *did* sound sort of cool. Finally, he sighed.

"Lucy, that's—"

"A horrible idea?"

"—brilliant!" he cried. "That would be perfect for you!"

"You think so?"

He nodded. "Sure. You're wonderful at giving advice.

And colleges love students who write for their school papers. If you could manage to write a big investigative piece that exposes lies and corruption somewhere, that would be great, too, but the advice column works." He walked over and hugged me. "Terrific choice. I'm very proud of you."

I wondered how colleges felt about pseudonyms.

I'd worry about that later. First I had to *get* the job.

I was a nervous wreck over the next few days. As Alan and Mom got more and more excited about the idea (obviously, it had been the first announcement on the agenda during family dinner), I got more and more nervous that the Advice Column Committee would decide to give the position to Cristina. The idea of Cristina beating me was bad enough, but the idea of letting Alan down felt even worse.

Finally, Cristina and I got called down to Dr. Rem-Wall's office. Unlike Justin Twersky, who was in there a lot because he was always getting in trouble for getting his tongue caught in the pencil sharpener and trying to glue the flaps of his ears to his neck, I had never been in there. I had heard from Alice that it was big (she had been called down there after the three-strikes texting law), and for the first time in her life, she wasn't exaggerating. It was *huge*. Not only were there two couches and a big-screen TV, but there was a ginormous painting of the school that took up almost the entire wall. You couldn't exactly tell that it was the school from the colorful blobs and squiggles, but the sign next to it that said PORTRAIT OF THE CENTER FOR CREATIVE LEARNING BY MARCUS MIRABELLE gave it away. He was a super-famous artist whose work was in museums, but because his daughter Clarabelle was an eighth grader at the school, he had done it for free. (The rumor was that he had given it to the school after Clarabelle almost got kicked out for "behavioral problems." Which, if you were forced to go through life with a name like Clarabelle Mirabelle, was understandable.)

"Lucy, since 'Annie' has designated you her representative to protect her secret identity, we've asked you here with Cristina today because the Advice Column Committee has reviewed the answers to the sample question we prepared," Dr. Rem-Wall began. "And after much deliberation they've come up with a decision as to who the new columnist will be."

I hadn't realized until that moment that a person could sweat behind their *knees*. I was so nervous that I couldn't stop fiddling with my new purple cowboy hat (Laurel had bought it for me as a good-luck charm that weekend) to the point where it flipped right off and into Dr. Rem-Wall's lap. "Whoops. Sorry," I said as she handed it back to me.

Cristina smiled. "Oh, Dr. Remington-Wallace. Thank

you so much for this incredible honor," she said in a voice so sweet it made my teeth hurt. "My parents think this is going to look so great on my school records—"

"Not so fast, Cristina," Dr. Rem-Wall said. "The new advice columnist is Annie."

"Wait a minute—WHAT?!" Cristina and I said at the same time. I couldn't believe it.

"But . . . how is that possible?" Cristina asked, dazed.

"Yeah," I said, equally dazed. Sure, I had wanted to be chosen, but I hadn't thought it would actually *happen.*

Dr. Rem-Wall reached for a file with a label that said COMMITTEE FINDINGS—ADVICE COLUMNIST. "I'll tell you how that's possible," she said as she took out two sheets of paper and laid them side by side. One I recognized as mine, even though it was typed out (I didn't want to risk anyone recognizing my handwriting). The other one I could tell was Cristina's because it was written in the same super-curly, super-girly handwriting that had ruined many kids' days with lines like "You know, there are these things called showers . . . maybe you'd like to take one," in notes that were passed to them during class.

Dr. Rem-Wall cleared her throat. "So, Lucy, 'Annie' may not have told you, but the sample question was '*Dear Advice Giver: Over the last few months, one of my classmates has started some rumors about me that have made it so that I'm constantly being teased at school. What should I do? Signed, Miserable in Manhattan,*'" she read.

You could tell that an adult had written the question because a real kid would've given you a lot more of the story. Like, say, was this an ex-BFF? What kind of rumors? Are they so bad that you have to hide in the bathroom during lunch and cry?

"And Annie's answer was '*Dear Miserable, Being teased is bad enough, but when untrue rumors are being spread it can get really serious,*'" Dr. Rem-Wall went on. "'*Like so serious, I'm not even going to try and make a joke here, which is what I sometimes tend to do when giving advice in order to lighten things up. And I'm not going to tell you to go talk to her about it as if she's a normal human being because we both know that that's going to be a waste of time. Instead, my advice is to get an adult involved. Like a teacher or a guidance counselor. Or if you have an awesome principal like I do, her. Don't worry that you're being a tattletale or anything, because you're not. Good luck, Annie*'" She put the paper down and smiled at us. "Now *that* is a very thoughtful and responsible answer."

I smiled back. The part about the principal was a bit butt-kissy, but Beatrice made me put it in. "Thanks. I mean . . . as Annie's official representative, I'll be sure to tell her you said that about the answer that she came up with herself that I had nothing to do with."

Was it my imagination or did Dr. Rem-Wall wink at me? As she picked up Cristina's reply, her smile disappeared. "And the other answer was '*Dear Whatever-Your-Name-Is: Talk about a simple answer. Just start some rumors about her! No offense or anything, but I can't believe you couldn't figure this out yourself. Signed, Cristina the Great.*'"

Cristina smiled. "The Cristina the Great thing is catchy, isn't it? My mom came up with it."

"No, Cristina, it's not," Dr. Rem-Wall replied. "And neither is your advice to poor Miserable in Manhattan. In fact, it's completely irresponsible, and I'm appalled that you would even *think* such a thing, let alone commit it to writing—"

"But Miserable in Manhattan doesn't even exist!" she cried. "It's a made-up person!"

"That's beside the point, Cristina," Dr. Rem-Wall snapped. "But what happened here is completely within the realm of possibility. Do you know how many years it takes to get kids to stop calling you Smelly Sally?"

"Who's Smelly Sally?" Cristina asked.

"It's not important," Dr. Rem-Wall said quickly.

Wait a minute—Dr. Rem-Wall's first name was Sally.

"The point is that here at the Center, we're all about honest communication," she went on. "And spreading rumors about people does not fall into that category."

"Maybe it's not honest, but it *is* communicating!" Cristina said.

"Not in my book," Dr. Rem-Wall said. "And not in

the books of the committee members. Which is why they unanimously voted that Annie will be the new columnist." She turned to me. "Will you take care of telling her, Lucy?"

"Who?" I asked.

"Annie."

"Oh right. Sure." Jeez. I really needed to force myself to remember that I was Annie. Or Annie was me. Or whatever. I nodded. "Sure."

"I have a feeling she'll do a great job with the column," Dr. Rem-Wall added. Either she had something in her eye, or she was winking at me again.

"Thanks," I said, relieved.

Finally, I—Lucy B. Parker—had an official hobby!

chapter 4

Dear Dr. Maude,

Okay, yes, I know I told you in my last e-mail that you wouldn't be hearing from me again. And I guess sending you this e-mail now technically makes that a lie, but I really WASN'T going to e-mail you, so it's not like I KNEW I was lying when I said that. I try to avoid lying whenever possible because it's so rough on your karma. Hold on—I'm going to add that to my advice notebook.

Okay, I'm back. Anyway I won't go into all of it now, because it's kind of a long story, but this is the deal: after dinner I called a special emergency meeting of Operation Annie. Beatrice came up to my apartment and we Skyped Laurel because she was at the studio where her show shoots. (You're probably saying to yourself "Who the heck is Annie?" but when I'm done with this story, that question will be answered.) And in the special emergency meeting, I got them to agree to let me tell you what's happening on account of the fact that it's now very obvious that I need some expert advice if I'm going to pull this thing off. (I know you're probably saying to yourself "What 'thing' is she talking about?" but don't worry—when I'm done with this story, that question will be answered, too.)

Okay, so this is what's happening . . . See, "Annie" just happens to be me. And "Annie" was just chosen to be the new advice columnist for the school paper! Which means (a) I kind of now have a job, and (b) more important, I have a hobby, which makes Alan super-happy.

I didn't tell you all this before because I was afraid you might get a little freaked out that I was going to be competition, but it turns out that I'm actually REALLY good at this advice-giving thing. And that's not just me being all full of myself and saying that, or Laurel saying that because she happens to be my frister and the one responsible for getting me into this mess in the first place. That's from all the kids who read the column when it came out in the school paper the other day with the sample questions that Laurel had come up with and said, "Hey, this Annie girl is REALLY good at this giving-advice thing." We're talking at least thirty-two kids! That's how many Alice and Malia counted during their eavesdropping during Operation Find-Out-Who-Likes-Annie. (In this case, because they had to get up so close to hear, it was actually eavesdropping. But just to be clear, what I do at home is overlistening. There's a difference.)

At first I wasn't going to tell Alice that I was Annie because she's such a huge blabbermouth, but after having to listen to her say for the hundredth time, "I'm so dying to know who Annie is, aren't you?!" I broke down and told her. Well, I told her after making her swear on Marshmallow's life (that's her little yippy bichon frise's name—because he's all white and puffy-looking) that she wouldn't tell anyone. And that if she did, then it would be perfectly okay for me to tell everyone that when she was at her cousin's wedding in North Carolina over the summer, she ended up sitting on a chair where someone had left an unwrapped candy bar and it exploded all over her butt and she didn't find out until she got back to her hotel that night.

So because I'm so good at this advice thing, I've received a bunch of real letters from people who need advice. Today alone I got ten of them! I know that's probably nowhere near the amount that you get on a daily basis (which explains why you don't get back to people—like, say, me—in a timely manner), but for someone who's only twelve years old, that's kind of a lot.

But here's my question. A lot of these letters have to do with things that I don't have any experience with. Like being freaked out about getting your first less-than-100-percent on a math quiz. (I think if I ever got anything above an 85 my mom would faint.) Or what to do to get your hair to stop growing so fast (I'd kill for that problem). Or the best place in the city to go skateboarding (for someone who's coordination challenged? Not so important).

So I'm not sure what to do—I mean, I don't want to lie and make something up and give bad advice that somehow ruins their life, but I also don't want to have to write "Ummm . . . you know, I don't really know the answer to that. Why don't you try Googling it?"

From the bio on your website, I know that you're a

"well-rounded individual with numerous hobbies" (BTW—I'd like to pick your brain about the hobby thing later on, if that's okay, because even though I finally have one myself, I was thinking I should have some backups as well). But even so, I'm sure that at least once or twice, someone has come to you with a problem that you don't have experience with, right? If you could give me advice on how to handle that, I'd sooooo appreciate it.

You may have ignored my other e-mails, but I'm really hoping that you'll answer this one because now we're not just talking about MY life. We're talking about the lives of A LOT of people here—an entire school. And I don't want you feeling super-guilty if something bad happens because I don't handle this the right way. Plus, there's the whole fellow-advice-columnist bond we now have.

Thanks so much.

yours truly,
LUCY B. PARKER

Usually when Laurel and I had an IBS, we went to a thrift store. Or the movies. Or to various drugstores around the city to track down the Bonne Bell Lip Smackers we didn't have yet in our collections. But Laurel had recently discovered in therapy that being a huge megastar had made her lose out on a lot of Regular Girl activities in her life (um, hello, I could've told her that for free). So she had put Operation Regular Girl into effect. Which meant that all her free time was now spent doing things she had never done before because she was too busy being a star. Like bowling at Lucky Strike Lanes downtown. And riding bikes through Central Park. And collecting money for UNICEF by knocking on our neighbors' doors (even though it wasn't Halloween).

And because she didn't have any Regular Girl friends other than me, I was forced to do Regular Girl things with her. But when she chose American Girl Place as her IBS pick, I had to put my foot down. Especially when she said she wouldn't wear one of her disguises because that would defeat the whole Regular Girl thing.

"American Girl Place?! But that's for eight-year-olds!" I cried.

"But I was busy going to the Kidz TV Awards when I was eight," she replied. "I totally missed out. You know, I realized in therapy the other day that that was about the time when I started wiping down the blinds in my bedroom every day."

Laurel had this annoying habit of not only cleaning the dust from her own window blinds, but from the rest of the bedrooms, too.

"So you think that if you had done more Regular Girl things, you wouldn't be so neat and organized?"

She shrugged. "Maybe."

Huh. I kind of *liked* the idea of her being less neat. That way my messiness wouldn't stand out so much.

"Come on, it'll be fun. Look at it this way—if anyone writes a letter asking for advice about American Girl dolls, you'll be able to give it to them."

This was true. Although I wasn't sure I'd be able to help anyone who was still interested in American Girl dolls at our age. "Okay—we'll go. But don't blame me when you have a hundred eight-year-olds begging for your autograph."

Try two hundred.

Talk about humiliating. And to make things worse, Mom decided to completely invite herself because she thought that "having the three women of the family do this kind of thing together is a lovely symbol of sisterhood," even though I wasn't technically a woman yet on account of the fact that I hadn't gotten my period yet. As Beatrice said when I texted her about it, that part was "TRES TRES TRES mortifying." *Tres* means "very" in French.

In the middle of the chaos, Mom grabbed hold of both of our hands so that we were standing in a little circle. Kind of like we were either about to say grace or play Ring Around the Rosie.

I could feel myself turning red. "Um, Mom? What are

you doing?" I whispered as one girl poked her friend and pointed at us.

"I'd like us to just have a Moment, please," she announced.

Oh no. Mom + a-Moment-with-a-capital-M = not good. In fact, any parent + Moments = potentially really, really bad. I had the kind of parents who were very into "sharing feelings and emotions." They *loved* a good Moment.

I could've lived with it if these Moments took place at home—like in the kitchen or living room with the drapes closed—but the thing about Moments was that, a lot of times, parents ended up choosing very public places for them to happen. Like, say, the hallway of my school in Northampton after my chorus concert, in front of the band kids, where my dad announced how, even though Ms. Edut, my chorus teacher, had asked me to mouth the words because I was such a bad singer, he was still incredibly proud of me. Or the feminine products aisle of CVS in front of one of the guys who worked there when Alan said that, even though he wasn't my biological father, he hoped I knew that I could talk to him about anything—even periods. Or the lobby of the Cinemark at Hampshire Mall movie theater when Mom went on and on about how grateful she was that I was still willing to spend Quality Time with her on a Friday night while Rachel and Missy, my two ex-BFFs, giggled in the corner, making me feel like even more of a loser than I already did.

"Can we have this Moment at home later, please?" I whispered. It was one thing to be humiliated in front of your ex-BFFs—it was a whole other thing to have it happen in front of a group of little girls holding creepy-looking dolls.

Mom cleared her throat and squeezed our hands. Apparently not. "I don't know what wonderful things I did in past lifetimes to be graced with such a magnificent daughter as Lucy," Mom began.

She had to bring up the past-lifetimes thing *now*? Sure, because of the Buddhism thing, I was used to it, but to the rest of the world, it sounded pretty weird. Like, the security guard who gave her a weird look.

"But with the addition of Laurel into our lives this past year, to now be blessed with *two* incredible daughters . . . well, that's just an embarrassment of riches."

Um, how about just an embarrassment *period*? I looked over at Laurel, who didn't seem the least bit humiliated. Which was either because (a) she was such a good actress, or (b) she didn't know enough about Regular Girlism to know it was completely okay to feel like your mother was being a freak. Yes, I was lucky to have a mom who paid more attention to me than her BlackBerry, which is what Alice's mom did, but still, if Mom started to cry (something that often happened during Moments), I was going to have to do something about it.

"I remember thinking back in college that if I ever ended up having a daughter, I would try my hardest not to project any of my unlived dreams upon her so that she could grow up to be her own person."

Laurel and I looked at each other. What the heck did that mean?

As Mom folded us in close to her—so close that it made me think that maybe she had forgotten to put deodorant on that morning—she started to tear up. "Laurel, I know that I can never take the place of your mom, but I hope you know that I love you just as much as if I had given birth to you myself."

Laurel managed to unstick her face from Mom's chest and look at her. "You do?" she asked. Because Laurel is the type of person who cries at most commercials—even non-animals-who-need-to-be-adopted ones—she was all teary, too.

"Absolutely," Mom replied. "And you have no idea how much joy it brings me and your father to see how close you and Lucy have become."

Okay, I *wasn't* the type of person who cried at commercials (other than the animal ones), but even *I* could feel a tear or two trying to squeeze its way out of my eye as I thought about how glad I was to have Laurel as my frister.

"To think of where you two are now," she continued,

"as opposed to that first day you met, with the Hat Incident..."

My eyes widened. Did she really have to go ahead and bring up one of the most embarrassing afternoons of my *life*? She *knew* how hard I had tried to block that memory out! "Mom!" I yelped. "Talk about ruining a Moment!"

She laughed and ruffled my hair. "Oh sweetie, but look at how much has *changed* since that day! Your hair growing back after you burned it off with the straightening iron—" she said. I cringed and pulled down my denim newsboy cap. Great. Yet another memory I had no interest in thinking about. "Laurel getting over her phobia of germs now that she's spent so much time with you—"

At that, Laurel turned red and slumped down a little herself. I felt bad that Mom was embarrassing her, too, but I had to admit it was nice to be in it together.

"It's wonderful that the two of you get to learn from each other like that," she went on. "You know, back when I was an adolescent—"

Parent + Moment + any sentence that started with "Back when I was an adolescent..." = DEFINITELY not good.

I wiggled out of Mom's embrace. "Hold on a second," I said as I fumbled in my bag. "I just need to write something down." I took out my advice notebook.

"*When a parent says it's time for a Moment . . . RUN!!!*"
I wrote. I looked back up at her. "Um, Mom, Laurel
and I would love to hear about what it was like back
when you were an adolescent"—now that I thought
about it, I don't think I had ever heard anyone use
"adolescent" in a conversation other than Mom—"but
do you think we could maybe wait until we get *home*
for you to do that? So we're in the *privacy* of our
apartment?"

"Of course, sweetie," she said, finally letting go of our
hands. "In fact, maybe I'll dig out my old photo albums,
make a big bowl of popcorn, and—"

"That sounds awesome!" Laurel said. "It's so . . .
regular-person-like!"

I sighed and uncapped my pen again: "*And when a
superstar decides she wants to be a Regular Girl, try and
talk her out of it,*" I wrote.

If I got any letters about embarrassing parents or
fristers, I was all set on that front.

Luckily, no moment lasts forever. Even if it's a Moment-
with-a-capital-M moment. And no visit to American Girl
Place lasts forever, either. Especially when some mom
tweets that Laurel Moses is there, and the store is flooded
with women and children and paparazzi, and you have
to be escorted by security to the manager's office and

told—very nicely—to please leave before more dolls get trampled.

"That was so fun!" Laurel said as we walked up Fifth Avenue afterward. "Well, at least until we were kicked out." She turned to Mom. "Hey, do you think maybe one weekend we can all go to Disney on Ice's Princess Classics?" she asked. "I saw that it's coming to Madison Square Garden."

This was getting out of control. My grandmother had taken me to Disney on Ice . . . *when I was six*. So what if Laurel was neat? And had officesupplygeek. com bookmarked on her computer? I could live with that stuff. But Laurel was so into being a Regular Girl now that I could barely ever get her to do regular teen superstar things like send an e-mail to the Bonne Bell company saying that she was a huge fan of their delicious Lip Smackers and would they happen to know where she could get more of the Cotton Candy ones in New York City because everywhere she had gone, they were sold out. (My hope was that because she was who she was, they would say, "We'll just send you a few for free!")

"Sure, sweetie," Mom replied. "I'll look into tickets as soon as your dad and I figure out where to go for our anniversary."

I cringed and tried not to get so nauseated that I upchucked the honey-roasted nuts I had just bought from one of the street vendors. The idea of them alone in a hotel was just gross.

"Trying to figure this out is harder than peace talks in the Middle East," she sighed. "Maybe when we get home I'll look on that woman Dr. Maude's website to see if she has any advice about what to do when you and your partner can't decide on where to go for a weekend away. In fact, I think I saw a link where you can send her an e-mail."

Oh no. That was *not* a good idea. Mom and Alan knew I was a big fan of the show, but they knew nothing about my e-mails to Dr. Maude. It wasn't like I was doing anything wrong, writing to her. But I was worried that Mom's feelings might be hurt if she found out that I was going to Dr. Maude for advice on stuff. It's not like you could blame me—Dr. Maude was a trained professional, and Mom, although she read a ton of self-help books, was not.

I know Dr. Maude hadn't answered even *one* of my e-mails, but what if, for some reason, she answered Mom's? And somehow it came up that Mom had a daughter named Lucy B. Parker and Dr. Maude would think to herself, Lucy B. Parker, Lucy B. Parker . . . where have I heard that name before? And she'd be so curious she'd go back into her e-mail in-box and she'd discover that she had a ton of unread e-mails from someone with that name? And then she'd TELL MOM that I had been writing her all this time, and

Mom would be all hurt, and she'd schedule a Talk with a Capital T between the two of us on the family schedule that was kept in the kitchen near the phone. And during the TWACT she'd say that she was disappointed because she had thought I knew I could tell her anything, and I'd say that for the most part I did. And then she'd ask if I wanted to go to therapy like she and Alan and Laurel and Beatrice did. And I'd say no, even though for a split second I'd consider it because maybe it could be considered a second hobby. And then it would turn into a Moment with her getting all cry-y, and I'd make a mental note to myself that if I wrote to Dr. Maude again, it would be with a pseudonym.

"Oh, I don't think that's a good idea," I said quickly.

"Why not? You love Dr. Maude!" Mom said.

"Yeah, but I heard she's really bad at answering e-mails." That wasn't exactly a lie. Other than leaving out the "I heard" and putting in a "my" in front of "e-mails," it was totally the truth.

"I know—you should ask Annie!" said Laurel.

As Mom and I looked at each other, I shrugged. Why not? The kids at my school were happy with the advice I had given them. In fact, Laurina Gibbs had been so happy with the answer I gave her about what to do when you had a pet who seemed to hate you (ramp up Operation Get a New One was my response) that her

Facebook status update yesterday was "Laurina thinks the Ask Annie advice column in her school newspaper is the best thing ever."

"Good idea," Mom said. She turned to me "So, Annie, any thoughts?"

My stomach started to get a little jumpy. It was one thing to come up with an answer to a kid's question in the privacy of my own bedroom (I had recently found that I came up with some of my best answers while doing headstands against the wall, which, according to Alice, was also supposed to help bring on your period). But to answer right in front of the person who needed advice? That was a whole other story. "Um, would you mind phrasing it in the form of a question?" I asked. "Because that's how I'm used to doing this, it'll help me get into character more."

"Sure. Okay. 'Dear Annie—I need some advice. Just to give you some background about myself, I'm a forty-seven-year-old woman living in New York City. I was born in—'"

"Mom, you don't have to start that far back," I said. "You can just tell me the question you need advice about."

"Oh. Okay. Well, then. . . let's see . . . 'Dear Annie, I'm trying to plan a weekend away with my partner but—' No, wait, I don't like the way that sounds. Let me start over."

I sighed. Mom was a writer, so she was always

rewriting. She had been working on her latest novel for seven years, and it still wasn't done. We could be here for a while, waiting for her to compose a fake letter in her head, and I'd miss this special on Animal Planet about animals that no one liked, called *Jackals Deserve Love, Too.*

Luckily, Laurel knew about Mom's writing problem and jumped in. "How about this? 'Dear Annie, I love my partner very much, and while we have no trouble deciding on what comedy to see on a Saturday night, when it comes to planning a weekend away, it turns into a horror movie. The fact that I love the country and he likes the city is making me feel like I need a vacation from planning a vacation! Signed, Baffled in the Big Apple.'"

I turned to her. "Wow, Laurel, that's *awesome*. If you ever get bored of acting, you could totally have a new career writing fake advice column letters! I can't believe you were able to come up with that so quickly on the spot."

She smiled. "Thanks. I think that improv class I took last year really helped."

Mom nodded. "I couldn't have said it better myself." She looked at me. "So, Annie, any advice?"

I took a deep breath and closed my eyes. Okay, I could do this.

"'Dear Baffled,'" I began, "'because I'm a kid, I have

to spend my vacations going where my parents take me because they're the ones paying for it, so I don't have experience with this *exact* thing, but I do know what it's like when you can't agree with someone on where to go for an after-school snack.'" I opened my eyes to see if they were still listening. When I saw that they were, I closed them again.

"'As far as I'm concerned, the best thing to do is just take charge and plan it yourself, with the plan just *happening* to include the place you want to go, and then *surprise* them with your plan. That way, they'll be all touched that you took the time to plan something, AND you'll get what you want, even though they'll be too touched to realize it.'" I opened my eyes again to find Mom's left eyebrow lifted, which was Momese for "Hmm ... I'm not sure I buy that." I closed them again.

"'*OR*,'" I went on, "'(b) if you're the kind of person who's worried about karma, you could plan a trip to a place you know they'd like. That way, you're not only a really nice person, but when you get into this position again, you can say, "Remember how last time we went to where you wanted to go? Well, because of that, it's only fair that this time we go where *I* want."'" I opened my eyes to find her cocking her head and holding her chin, which was Momese for "Hmm ... I like that."

"Hmm ... I like that," she said.

I turned to Laurel, who nodded in agreement. "Really impressive. I know the advice thing is your hobby now, but I think you should consider taking an improv class. I bet you'd be great at it."

I smiled. "Thanks, you guys."

Mom nodded. "I *really* like this idea," she said. "I think what I'll do is book a room at 60 Thompson down in Soho, and get us tickets to a Broadway play—maybe even a musical because Alan likes those so much, even though I find them hard to sit through—and we'll have brunch at Locanda Verde in Tribeca and—" She smothered me in a hug. "Oh, Lucy, what great advice! Thank you so much!"

"You mean Annie," I said into her chest.

"Annie, Lucy, whoever you are—you're *brilliant*!"

Maybe I really *was* good at this. I mean, having to come up with something on the spot was a little scary, but it wasn't *that* bad. In fact, if I ended up doing it enough, it might feel so normal that one day I, too, could have a show like Dr. Maude! Or at least fill in for her as a guest host while she went on vacation.

Not to mention that when Alan and Mom were hanging out in their hotel room (after having Done It—*eww!*), and Alan said, "Rebecca, this is such a wonderful surprise, and I appreciate it *so* much. How did you ever come up with such a great idea?" Mom would say,

"Actually, I ended up asking Lucy for advice, and *she* was the one who came up with it."

Which would make Alan realize that not only did I have a hobby, but that Laurel wasn't the only kid in the family with talent.

chapter 5

Dear Dr. Maude,

Remember when I told you that it seems like I might be kind of good at this advice-giving thing? Well, it turns out that I'm REALLY good at it! Not only am I—I mean, Annie—getting more and more letters from the kids at school, but the other day I was able to help Mom solve her problem about where she and Alan should go for their weekend away (BTW, have you ever thought about the idea of talking about karma on your show? Not to tell you how to do your job or anything, but when dealing with my clients, I find that when you bring karma up, they get all worried that if they don't follow your advice, it's going to screw up the rest of their lifetimes).

But as busy as I am helping people solve their problems, and as much as I try not to think about my own problem, it's still there. Not only that, but with every day it's just getting bigger and bigger. And I'm not talking about my boobs, or the fact that I now have so many boxes of unopened maxipads in my closet that when I opened the door the other day they toppled over and fell out. I'm talking about the thing that I need advice about that I now feel bad asking you for advice about because we're now rivals. You know, the B.L.M (Blair Lerner-Moskovitz) thing.

Which brings me to you. Sure, I could have written to Sara, from that "Sara Says . . ." column in *Fifteen* magazine. Or Alisa from "Advice from Alisa" in *Teens Today*.

Actually, I DID write to them. But what I got back from both of them was an e-mail saying, "Due to the heavy volume of letters received, please be advised that your letter may not be answered." Which is why I thought I'd give you another try.

See, the Sadie Hawkins dance is only ten days away. Actually, it's nine days, seven hours, and forty-three minutes away. Which, when you don't have the guts to ask anyone—let alone your local crush—because you'd either have to die or at least throw up if they said no, isn't a lot of time.

Although I will say that I just saw on the A&E website that they're having a *Hoarders* marathon that night, and I really don't want to miss it. Sure, I could TiVo it, but because I'm so busy with all my advice giving, it's hard to find time to watch TiVo'd shows.

I know you haven't answered any of my other

e-mails, but if you could just answer this one and let me know, I'd really appreciate it.

Thanks.

yours truly,
LUCY B. Parker

While I waited for Dr. Maude to write me back (I figured it had to happen at *some* point), I decided to see if Skyping with Ziggy when it wasn't nap time would net me some advice.

"Hey Zig, *que pasa*?" I yelled into the computer. "That means 'what's up' in Spanish." Pete, who was Puerto Rican, said it to me all the time. Back when Sarah was pregnant I had gotten annoyed at how Dad was all into making sure Ziggy turned out super-genius-y. But now that it was obvious he was so smart, I figured I'd do my part to teach him what I could. "Can you say '*que pasa*'?"

He put his little lips together and made a raspberry sound.

"Okay. We'll work on that some other time," I said. "So Ziggy—I need some more advice."

He laughed.

"Hey, it's not my fault I have one of those lives where

there's a lot going on. So about that dance I told you about last time—"

He gave a little sigh.

"Yeah. That again," I sighed back. "Believe me, I'm sick of it, too. Anyway, the thing is, I'm running out of time. I know I still haven't told Beatrice or anything, but once I do, then I still have to ask Blair."

Ziggy covered his eyes.

"I know! That's how I feel about it, too!" I exclaimed. It was probably because we were related, but it was kind of crazy how Ziggy and I tended to think exactly the same way. "So do you have any advice about how to do it? Not like I'm definitely *going* to, but if I did?"

At first Ziggy was so quiet I wondered if he had fallen asleep again. Which is why I leaned in close to the computer and yelled "ZIGGY? ARE YOU SLEEPING?" But I could see from the way his eyes were open and he kept trying to stick his fingers in his nose that he was awake.

I sighed. "Can you just give me *something*, Ziggy?"

And then he did. Because right then he screwed his eyes up tight, and I heard something that sounded like a shaken-up soda can exploding after being opened.

I cringed as I picked up my phone to text Dad that it seemed that someone needed his diaper changed. And fast.

I had hoped it wouldn't get to this point, but I realized I had no choice. I still needed advice.

It was time to set up another Skype session.

This time, a Triple-S one.

Connor Forrester was the one who came up with the actual idea for the Skype Snack Session, aka Triple S. Before I had met him I never would've thought that we could've been friends. He was really cute . . . and a big star . . . and really cute . . . and a big star. But we got along really well, and he made me laugh a lot. Plus, he was the first (and only) boy I had ever kissed. And even though I didn't *like* him like-him, we were friends.

You'd think that someone who was as big of a star as Connor would be all stuck-up and full of himself and think that everything he had to say was super-important, like on the level of Dr. Maude, but that wasn't the case. In fact, the more I got to know him, the more I discovered that—like Laurel—he could be just as nervous and unsure of himself as *un*famous people.

After I got back to New York, we got into this thing where once a week we would Skype while eating a snack at the same time (that's where the name came from). Because we could see each other on the computer, it was almost like hanging out in person, but the good news was (a) we didn't have to worry about the paparazzi taking pictures of us, and (b) I didn't have to worry about whether my breath smelled from Doritos.

Connor was shooting his new movie, *Monkeyin' Around*, in Mexico (his last seven movies had starred chimps or apes or orangutans), so his schedule had been a little crazy lately, but when I texted him: *Need an emergency Triple S NOW!!!*, he immediately texted me back: *Give me 5 min—need to wash monkey slobber off.*

"So what's going on, dudette?" he asked a few minutes later as we snacked away. I tried not to have snack envy, but it was hard. While I crunched away on a bag of boring old pita chips, I could see that he had a whole spread of fun foods such as trail mix, Nutter Butter cookies, and chocolate-covered raisins. Squinting, I saw that there even seemed to be some gummi worms there. Obviously, he had hit the craft services truck before going to his trailer.

Craft services was this place they had on TV and movie sets that was full of tons of different foods that you could take as much of as you wanted for free. Which, because movie stars made so much money, seemed a little unfair.

"Well, I kind of need your advice about something," I began.

"A big-time advice columnist like you needs *my*

advice?!" he exclaimed. When I had e-mailed Connor about my column, he was really impressed. "Dude, that is *so* cool!"

I rolled my eyes. "Connor—"

"Sorry—I mean dud*ette*." Even though he definitely knew I was a girl on account of the kiss thing, he always called me "dude." "It's just that I can't believe you're coming to *me* for advice!"

"Yeah. Okay, so, um, see, there's this. . . . ah—" I sputtered. Uh-oh. This was going to be tough. In fact, as I felt the sweat begin to bead on my forehead, I moved back from the webcam.

And I realized it was going to be even harder when Connor picked up the guitar that was next to him on the couch in his trailer and started to strum it while I tried not to cringe. During one of our Triple S's, he had admitted to me that one of his dreams was to start a singing career, like Laurel's. What I wanted to say—but didn't, on account of the fact that it would've been mean—was that, unlike Laurel, he didn't actually have any singing talent. In fact, if he had been just a regular kid, and had Ms. Edut for chorus, she would've told *him* to mouth the lyrics, too.

"There's this what?" he asked.

I mopped my forehead with my sleeve. "Hold on a second—I'm trying to get my thoughts together!" I cried.

He shrugged. "Okay, then while you get your thoughts together, let me play you this new song I just wrote. It's called *Pizza Guy Blues*—"

"Uh, no, that's okay, they're together now," I said quickly. In our last Triple S, he insisted on playing a song called "*Why Be Sad When You Have Wii*"? and it was so bad, I had to mute the volume on my computer until he was done. "Okay . . . well, it's kind of a long story, so I won't get into all of it right now, but the bottom line is this—" I took a deep breath and screwed my eyes shut tight. "I'mthinkingofaskingaboytoadance," I blurted out.

"Huh?"

"I *said* . . . I'mthinkingofaskingaboytoadance."

He leaned in so close to the webcam that all I could see were the insides of his nostrils. Luckily, there wasn't anything gross in there. "You're saying it too fast!" he yelled very loudly and slowly, like the way my grandmother talked to people who didn't speak English.

I rolled my eyes. Laurel and Beatrice didn't have any problem understanding me when I did that. I guess that's why they were my BFFs and Connor was just a boy. "I *said* . . . I'm. Thinking. Of. Asking. A. Boy. To. A. Dance." I braced myself for the lightning that I was sure was about to strike me, but nothing happened, other than Miss Piggy making the gagging noise she made right before she upchucked a hairball. Which I would clean up later, if I was still alive because I didn't die from embarrassment first.

"Not that I'm really interested in doing something like that," I added. "But it's in nine days, and it's a Sadie Hawkins dance, where the girls have to ask the boys, and because I'm class president I really should be there. So, you know, it looks like I'm taking my job seriously. I mean, I don't want to get impeached or anything like that. That would look really bad on my school record."

He turned red. "Wow, Lucy, that's really cool that you asked me . . . but I'm not going to be able to make it," he said nervously. "That's the same night that I'm hosting the 'Primates in Film' Awards."

Oh my God. Connor Forrester thought I was asking him OUT. To a DANCE. Which was like a DATE. This was beyond humiliating. Now it wasn't just my face or the backs of my knees that were sweating—my back had joined the party, too. "Actually, I wasn't—" I started to say.

"And, uh, there's something I've been meaning to tell you," he said. He took a deep breath. "And I guess now is as good of a time as any. You see, I've kind of been . . . hanging out with someone here."

My face paled. Oh great. Connor thought I *liked*-liked him! Which I SO did not. This was even more embarrassing than having to ask him for advice. "That's great," I said. "But that's not why I wanted to talk to you—"

"You're a really awesome girl, Lucy. Like totally, seriously, *beyond* awesome," he said. "I mean, you eat bread, for crying out loud, which is something barely anyone here in L.A.—guys or girls—do. And if we lived in the same city, I'd totally be into hanging out in, you know, *that* way, but with the distance and all—"

I got really close to the camera and microphone on the computer so that he wouldn't miss what I was about to say. I didn't even care if he could see up my nostrils. "Connor, I wasn't calling to ask you to the dance!" I yelled. "I was calling you for advice about how to ask a *different* boy!"

I pulled back to see him shielding himself with a pillow. "Whoa—take it down a few notches, Parker," he said. "I think you just blew my eardrum out."

"Sorry," I replied.

"So you weren't going to ask me to that Sally Hansen dance?" he asked, relieved.

"It's Sadie Hawkins," I corrected. Boy, that was a dumb name. Maybe that's why she had been forced to ask a boy—because of her name. I shook my head. "And, no, I wasn't."

He grinned. "Phew. What a relief." Then he looked confused. "Wait a minute—you weren't?" he asked, looking kind of hurt.

"No! And first of all, like I said, I'm only *thinking* of

asking someone," I corrected. "I didn't say I was going to ask him for sure."

"Oh. What's the second of all?"

"Huh?"

"You said 'first of all,' and usually when people say that, there's a second of all that comes after it."

I thought about it. "I'm not exactly sure what the second of all is, but I know there is one," I replied. "But that part doesn't matter. What matters is, if I *did* end up asking someone—not that I'm going to, but if I did— how would I do it?"

"Who would you ask if you did ask someone?"

"B.L.M," I whispered.

He got all close to the webcam again. "Who?!" he yelled.

I covered my ears. "If I asked someone it would be..." I took a deep breath. No use whispering it or else we'd be here all day. "Blair Lerner-Moskovitz!" I yelled.

"Wait a minute—are you talking about the guy in the *Chess Club*?"

I nodded.

"You're going to ask a dude who's in the *Chess Club* instead of me?" he asked, sounding all hurt.

I rolled my eyes. Once when I was overlistening, I heard Mom say to Deanna that all boys—no matter if they were seven or seventy-two—were total babies. At the time I wasn't sure what that meant, and it wasn't like

I could ask on account of the fact that I was supposed to be sleeping because it was close to midnight and I had school the next day. But now I realized what she was talking about. "Like I said, it's kind of a long story, so I won't go into all of it right now so just tell me how I would do it if I did it, okay?"

"Oh, that's easy," he said, kicking back and starting to strum his guitar again, very off-key. "You just go up to him and—"

"Wait! Wait!" I said, running to my bag to get my advice notebook and my purple pen. This might come in really handy if I ever received an advice question about how to ask a boy to a dance. "Okay, now I'm ready," I announced when I got back. "So I just go up to him and what?"

He stopped strumming and leaned in closer to the camera. "You really want to go with him instead of me? Really?" he asked, amazed.

I rolled my eyes again. "*Connor.* Can you just tell me?!" I asked.

"Okay, okay. So you just go up to him and you..." He stopped. "Chess Club? Dude, *really*?"

"Connor!" I was gripping the pen so hard by this point I was afraid I was going to snap it in two.

"Sorry. Okay. Anyway, so you just go up to him and you say, 'Hey Blair, so there's this dance thing at my school. You want to go?'"

I unclenched the pen. "That's it?"

He nodded.

"But . . . that's so . . . *simple*," I said.

He smiled. "Well, *yeah*. And then he'll either say, 'Sure, I'd love to' or he'll say 'Uh, that sounds cool but I can't because . . .' and he'll come up with some really lame excuse. And because you'll know he's lying because you girls have some sort of lie detector implanted in your skulls when you're born, you'll get all upset and go somewhere and cry for a while and then you'll just ask someone else. Like maybe someone who's in the . . . astronomy club."

"Are you sure it's that easy?" I demanded.

He nodded.

I sighed. Then why did it all seem so hard?

At least I wasn't the *only* chicken when it came to the dance. Judging from the number of letters Annie was getting, there were tons of us.

Later that afternoon I sat on the couch in the lobby with my laptop sorting through Annie's letters. Ever since Pete had just *happened* to mention that Dr. Maude was back in town after her countrywide book tour for her latest book *Everyone's Sick of Listening to You Whine—So JUST STOP IT!* I just *happened* to be hanging out in the lobby whenever I wasn't at school or asleep.

Some people might have considered that stalking, but my feeling was that stalking was more like pressing the person's floor number in the elevator at least five times a day so that when the doors opened, maybe you'd get a glimpse of them in the hallway. (And since I did that only three times a day, it wasn't stalking.) (Well, four a day on weekends.) (Fine, so one Sunday I did it five times. But it was just that one Sunday.)

"More e-mails about the dance?" Pete asked.

"Yeah," I sighed. "How'd you know?"

"From the eye roll," he replied. "It's different from the one you give when you're reading an e-mail from Marissa, or when Laurel's going on about some organizing system she wants to try."

"Wow. You can really tell the difference in my eye rolls?" I asked, impressed.

He *pfft*'d like he did whenever I asked a dumb question—like, say, "You really think V&T's has better pizza than Patsy's?"

"Of course I can tell the difference!" he replied. "You're one of my closest friends. Friends notice these type of things."

This was true. I could tell how freaked out Laurel was about having to look at my messy room from how much she scratched the inside of her arm. And how annoyed Beatrice was about something from how wide her nostrils flared.

"Plus, there's the whole doorman thing of it all," he added. "You know, 'cause—"

"—you're a doorman, and doormen know these things." I finished. That was another thing about friends— you could finish their sentences for them. Especially when they happened to say one particular sentence over and over.

"Exactly," he agreed. "So what's that e-mail say?"

"'Dear Annie,'" I read out loud. "'You know the Sadie Hawkins dance that's coming up in less than a week? Well, there's this boy I want to ask, but the problem is he recently broke his leg so he has a cast, which makes it so that he wouldn't be able to dance and we'd have to spend the night sitting on the bleachers talking. I already know him a little bit because we're lab partners, but a forty-minute science class is a lot different than having to come up with things to say for an entire evening. Do you have any advice for me? Sincerely, A girl who likes a boy with a cast.'" I looked at Pete. "She should've just written 'Sincerely, Ashley Robertson' because that's who it is."

"How do you know?" asked Pete.

"Because the boy she's talking about is Noah Kreisman," I replied. "He broke it when he fell down the escalator at the subway stop at Sixty-third and Lexington." Like me, Noah had coordination issues. Or . . . maybe he *didn't*. Maybe he was just *pretending* it was broken because he had a feeling Ashley was going to ask him and he knew she smelled like mothballs. *"Dear Ash—"* I said aloud as I typed. Then I stopped and deleted it. *"'Dear Cast Liker,'"* I wrote instead. *"Even though I don't know why you'd want to go to the dance when you could stay home that night and watch the* Hoarders *marathon on A&E—"*

Pete shook his head. "I dunno—I'm thinking that might sound too much like an editorial." We had recently learned about editorials in class. They were the part of the paper where people gave their opinions rather than just reporting the facts of a news story. And then people would write mean letters to the editor about them, saying the people who wrote the editorials were unhappy people who were big know-it-alls.

"Yeah, I guess you're right," I agreed as I pushed the delete key. *"'I think you should go ahead and ask him to the dance,'"* I typed. *"'Luckily for you, I have a lot of experience with having to talk to people who I'm worried I don't have a lot to talk about with.'"*

This was true—when Dad first started dating Sarah and he decided it would be a great idea if she and I spent a Saturday afternoon alone so we could have some Quality Bonding Time (sort of like Alan's IBSs, but not as organized, on account of the fact that Dad is a "creative type" because he's a photographer), I was really nervous that I wouldn't have much to say to her because she's so weird.

That day, as we sat across the table staring at each other at this vegetarian place where they only served gross stuff like tofu and tempeh, I realized I was right—I *didn't* have anything to talk to her about. Which is why I just asked her questions about herself, and let her talk. And talk. And talk. And before I knew it, it was time to go home, and I knew way more about yoga poses and essential oils than I ever needed to know.

"*'And what I've found is that if you're having trouble making conversation, just ask the person about themselves. Because it turns out that people LOVE to talk about themselves. Plus, by doing that, you get to see what they're really like. For instance, if they don't end up asking you about you at all, you probably don't want to be their friend, you know? So my advice is to ask Noah'*"—I stopped and deleted that last word—"'*the guy with the cast to the dance. Because not only will you get to see if he's selfish, but that way you won't have to worry about looking silly dancing in front of people. Which is the way I know I'd feel.*'" I looked at Pete. "How's that?"

He nodded. "It's pretty good. I think you have a real knack for this advice stuff. You know, if you ever wanted to look into a career as a doorwoman, I think you'd be real good at it."

I smiled. Coming from Pete, that was huge. "Thanks, Pete." I scrolled down. "Here's another one. '*Dear Annie,*'" I read, "'*I'm hoping you can help me.*

You've probably heard about this Sadie Hawkins dance thing, right?'" I rolled my eyes before realizing it was a form of editorializing. *"'If so, then you know the girls have to ask the boys. Well, I'm a boy, and there's this girl that I'm hoping will ask me. She sits in front of me in homeroom and we've had some really good conversations. (That is, if someone saying, "Do you have an extra pencil?," and you saying, "Sure," counts as a conversation?) But there's a problem . . . a few weeks ago I broke my leg, and now it's in a cast'"*—I looked up at Pete, my eyes wide—*"'so I'm afraid she won't ask me because it would be hard for me to actually dance,'"* I continued. *"'And I know that America's Worst Dancers is one of her favorite TV shows because I heard her talking about it one morning. How can I let her know that I'd like her to ask me and convince her that we'd have a really good time even if we couldn't take part in the dance part of the dance? Thanks in advance, Guy with a Broken Leg.'"*

I gasped. "Uh-oh. Noah's the only guy in the school with a cast."

"Well, that's good," Pete said. "Then this one's gonna have a happy ending."

I shook my head. "But the girl who sits in front of him isn't Ashley—it's *Romy Lucas*! *Now* what am I supposed to do?"

"Whattya mean what are you supposed to do?" he asked. "You give them advice, that's what you do. It's your job."

"Yeah, but this isn't your regular run-of-the-mill-how-do-I-get-out-of-cleaning-my-room question," I said. "This is complicated. It's like ... a word problem or something. And you know how I feel about math."

Pete shrugged. "Yeah, but when you took this gig, you took an *oath*—" he said.

I did? I didn't remember that part.

"—to be as helpful and honest as possible, no matter what your personal view is on the situation and how you feel about the person," he went on. "Like when you agree to walk someone's dog for a measly ten bucks a walk when they have more money than a small country, and then they try and stiff you on a tip when the holidays roll around," he grumbled.

I knew who he was talking about—Mrs. Spitzer in 17G. As rich as she was, she was that much cheaper. Beatrice said that the cheapness was the *reason* she was so rich. "Yeah, but what about the fact that because I know who all these kids are, I know that even though Ashley's a little on the boring side and she smells like mothballs, Noah would have a much better time at the dance with her because Romy's stuck-up and talks about people behind their backs? *Including* her best friend Caroline McNamara?"

He shrugged. "Yeah, but technically, you're not supposed to know who they all are. Which is why you just have to answer the question as if you didn't."

I sighed. Up until now, I hadn't cared that I wasn't

getting paid for this job, but now it felt like a whole different story. This was *hard*.

"'*Dear Broken Leg Guy,*'" I wrote. "'*What I tend to do in these types of situations where I want someone to know something but I don't want to say it directly is that I just sort of keep announcing things so that I know they'll hear it and hopefully get the point. For instance, the next time you're in homeroom, you could say, "Boy, I'd sure like to go to that Sadie Hawkins dance" REALLY LOUD. And then the next day you could say—again, REALLY LOUD—"Even if I can't dance at the moment because of my broken foot, I'd sure like to go to the Sadie Hawkins dance and TALK about dancing. Like, say, the dancing on* America's Worst Dancers, *which is one of my favorite shows." (But, if it's not one of your favorite shows, don't say that last part because that would be lying, which tends to bring you bad karma and probably wouldn't be helpful with this dance situation. So if that's the case, instead you could say something like ". . . which is a show that I haven't seen all that often but I have a feeling is really good, and I'm going to make an effort to watch more regularly.") Hopefully, if you keep doing that kind of thing on a daily basis, Romy*'*"—I stopped and deleted that part—"'*the girl you want to ask you to the dance will get the point and ask you. Oh, but when you're doing all that, try and make it sound natural, you know? Otherwise, it's* *going to be really obvious that you're trying to get her attention and plant an idea in her head, as if you're trying to brainwash her. I mean, yes, you ARE kind of trying to brainwash her, but she doesn't need to know that. Good luck, Annie.'"*

I looked up at Pete. "What do you think?"

He nodded. "That's excellent advice."

"I just want to add one last thing," I said. "'P.S.'" I typed. "*'Obviously you can do whatever you want, but just one more thing: I know you SAY that you want to go with the girl who sits in front of you in homeroom, but maybe there are some girls in your class who you might have an even better time with at the dance. Like, for instance, girls who you know from . . . science class. Maybe even girls who sit NEXT to you in science class. Just something to think about.'"* I looked up at Pete. "Is that okay?"

He started stroking his chin, which was not a good sign because it meant that he was going to start giving some long lecture. Usually, one that started with, "You know, Lucy, back when I was your age" which, because he was fifty, was almost a million years ago.

"You know, Lucy, back when I was your age—" he began.

"How come adults always say that?" came a voice from behind me. "Oh, hey, Lucy."

Uh-oh. I knew that voice. The one with the stuffed-up-nose-as-if-the-person-was-always-suffering-from-allergies-because-he-was sound. Did this really have to happen *now*?

I turned around. "Hey, Blair," I mumbled.

"Stalking Dr. Maude again?" he asked as he plopped down next to me on the couch and reached for a handful of my chocolate-covered pretzels without asking. He may have been my local crush, but that didn't mean he could take like *half the bag* in one grab. That was just rude.

"*No,*" I said. I knew that telling him about my letters to Dr. Maude had been a mistake. It's just that when you're hanging out in Central Park while shooting a video for your election, totally stuffed from hot dogs and papaya drinks from Gray's Papaya, you find yourself talking about things that you wouldn't normally bring up.

He gave me a look before using the corner of his T-shirt to swipe at the chocolate on the side of his face. Some people might have thought that was gross, but sometimes when I was alone and didn't feel like getting up to get a napkin, I did the same thing.

I felt myself turning red. "Okay, fine. If Dr. Maude walked by, would I introduce myself? Probably." I pointed to my computer. "But what I'm really doing is working."

"Did you hear that Lucy is the new advice columnist for her school paper?" Pete asked. "Except she's going by the name Annie to keep her identity a secret."

So much for the secret part being kept a secret.

"That's cool," Blair said, reaching for more pretzels. If

he took any more after that, I was going to have to seriously rethink whether I could possibly have a crush on someone so greedy. "What kind of questions do you get?"

I felt myself turning red. "Nothing interesting. Just questions about—" Questions about what? They were all about the dance, and there was no way I was bringing *that* up, even though it was the perfect opportunity.

"The dance that's coming up at her school in a week," Pete chimed in. "One where the girls have to ask the boys."

I gave him a look. What was he doing?!

"Yeah. Last night I walked past my sister's room and she was practicing asking some guy named Chris in front of her mirror." He snorted. "I can't *wait* to tease her about that."

Oh my God—that was *awful*! Even though that particular embarrassing thing had nothing to do with me, Beatrice and I were so close that my armpits started to sweat *for* her.

"Did you also know that Lucy hasn't asked anyone yet?" Pete added.

It had been nice being friends with Pete, but now I was obviously going to have to kill him. "That's because *I'm not sure I'm going*," I hissed.

"But you're class president," Blair said. "Won't it look weird if you're not there?"

"Well, I mean, I'm not going . . . as of yet," I sputtered.

I bit down on my lip to stop myself from bloversharing. "I mean, I *might* go. But I might not. It all depends on whether . . . or not I go. Which, as of right now, I'm not. But I might."

Pete cringed and shook his head. That wasn't even bloversharing. That was . . . I didn't even *know* what that was.

I stood up and started toward the elevator. "I have to go," I announced. "I just remembered I have to . . . go do something . . . that makes it so I have to go now," I sputtered nervously. It was only when I was safely in the elevator with the doors closed that I let out all the breath I was holding.

How could I ask Blair to the dance when I couldn't even have a two-minute conversation with him before having to run away?

chapter 6

Dear Dr. Maude,

Just in case you were wondering, this advice thing has gotten completely out of control.

Like so out of control that I can't even go into it at the moment.

yours truly,
LUCY B. PARKER

Some people (e.g., Alice and Marissa) tend to exaggerate a lot. Other people (e.g., me) do not. So when I said that it had gotten completely out of control, it had gotten completely out of control.

The out-of-control stuff started a few days after wimping out in front of Blair in the lobby. Because I didn't want to risk running into him so I could not ask him to the dance *again*—like in the elevator—I had started to take the stairs to and from our apartment.

Which, when you're talking twenty-one floors, makes up for an entire lifetime of missing gym.

I had just made it up and through the door and was wondering if I had done permanent damage to my legs because they felt like wiggly strands of spaghetti when I saw Alan pacing. Alan had a bunch of different pacing styles. When he was on the phone, he paced slowly. When he was thinking hard, he paced really fast. Those kinds of pacing didn't worry me. In fact, I found it to be kind of soothing—like when Mom tickled my arm when we were on the couch together watching TV.

But when he was really nervous or worried, his pacing was more like stomping, and included his rubbing the sides of his head. Not so soothing. In fact, it made *me* nervous. And if he was pulling at the little hair he had left while he paced? Really not good.

"What's wrong?" I asked nervously when I saw him stomping and pulling at his hair.

"It's this anniversary thing!" he cried. "We just can't seem to agree on where to go. And now your mom is so upset about the whole thing, she said we just shouldn't do *anything*!"

I knew that was Mom just trying to make the whole thing even more of a surprise, but *Alan* didn't know that, so it made sense that he was worried.

Well, because he was a worrier to begin with, more worried than usual.

He sighed. "It figures that Dr. Heath would choose *now* to go on a three-week vacation to India." Dr. Heath was Alan's therapist. And her cousin was Laurel's therapist. And her cousin's husband was Mom's therapist, but only as of two weeks ago. (When I had asked Mom why she was going to a therapist now, she said there wasn't any real reason other than it was "rite of passage when you lived in Manhattan"— kind of like taking the wrong train and ending up in Queens when you meant to go downtown, which was something I did when we first moved here.) So far I had managed to avoid having to go to a therapist, but Beatrice said that if I did go, I shouldn't worry because it wasn't so bad. She had been going to one since she was eight, so she would know ("When you're born into a family where you have two mothers or two fathers, I think there's a list of shrinks' names in the welcome kit they give you at the hospital"). She also said that some doctors had bowls of M&M's or Hershey's Kisses in their offices, so if possible, I should try to get one of those.

"I don't know who else to go to for advice on how to handle this," he said. Then he stopped pacing and looked at me. "Wait a minute—Lucy, have *you* ever gotten a letter about anything that's like this?"

Oh no. Alan was asking me for advice now?! While I had been hoping for an opportunity to prove to him how talented I was, now didn't seem like the greatest time. "Well, not really, because most kids I know other than Laurel don't have enough money saved up to plan a vacation, but I *do* have some experience with something similar to this," I replied. Actually, I had experience with the *exact* same question, but I couldn't tell Alan that because it would mean ruining the surprise.

"You do? So what's your advice?" he asked as the pacing began again.

While it may not have been the greatest time, I was pretty sure Pete would've said that, in that advice-giving oath I don't remember taking, I had pledged to give advice to anyone, at any time. "Well, the way I see it, there are two things you could do," I began nervously. "The first is that instead of coming up with something that the two of you might enjoy, you could just end up surprising the other person by planning a weekend at a place that they really like, even if you don't. Because, see, not only does that show that you really care about them, but it's really good for your karma. And the second is—"

At that, he stopped so short, he almost toppled over backward. "That's brilliant!" he cried. "That's what I'll do! I'll book the weekend at that place in Vermont I saw online the other day!"

Uh-oh. This was not good. That was what I'd told Mom! "No—wait!" I said. "There's a second thing. Remember I said there were two things you could do?!"

He started pacing again, but this time in his excited way instead of his worried way. "This will be great!" he exclaimed. "I think I saw on the website that it has a working farm. She'll *love* that!" He stopped. "The animals there have all had their rabies shots, don't you think?" he asked nervously.

"But there's a *second* thing," I said again. "And you should probably hear that part before making your decision. See, the other thing you could do is just wait and see if the *other* person ends up choosing a place . . . because they just might do that."

He walked over and hugged me. "You're right—I could," he said. "But I *love* that first suggestion. It's perfect. Sure, personally, I'd rather spend the weekend taking in a Broadway show, and staying at a nice hotel here in the city, but we can do that some other time. Your mom means the world to me, and if being surrounded by trees and farm animals and ticks that can cause Lyme disease will show her that, there's no reason why I can't make it through a weekend." He paused. "Or at least thirty-six hours."

What was I going to do?! I couldn't tell him that Mom was going to surprise him with the exact weekend that he wanted. But if he went ahead and booked a trip to Vermont for their anniversary, this was going to get really messy. "You know, Mom *says* she likes nature," I replied, "but I bet if you suggested that weekend you were talking about, with the hotel and the Broadway play, she'd like that just as much."

He shook his head. "She's so great, she'd *say* she was okay with it, but I don't think she'd enjoy it. That's more the kind of thing I'd like."

I sighed. Well, at least I knew my advice to Mom was spot-on.

He gave me another hug. "Lucy, you really *are* great at giving advice. I'm so proud of you."

I smiled. "You are?"

He nodded. "Very much so. Now, if you'll excuse me, I have a weekend at a farm to plan!"

It felt so good to hear him say that, it almost made me forget I had a major problem on my hands. The good news was that I had finally found something that made Alan proud of me. The bad news was that I was so good at it, it was going to screw up their anniversary weekend.

Now I needed advice about being great at giving advice.

Things got even more out of control the next day in science class.

"Hey, Lucy," Todd Olivera, my science lab partner, wheezed as he jabbed me in the shoulder blades while I tried not to let my coordination issues get in the way of pouring the water for our hydrogen experiment. Although if I had screwed up and somehow gotten electrocuted—even though Mr. Eagle Eye had sworn that wasn't possible when Olivia Barnett had raised her hand and asked that very question—I bet that would've got me out of (a) going to the dance, and (b) having to clean up the mess around Mom and Alan's anniversary.

"Yeah, Todd?" I asked, glancing over at Ashley and Noah at the next lab table. I wonder if she'd take my advice, which had appeared in that morning's paper, and ask him. I sure hope she did, before *he* took my advice and started talking about *America's Worst Dancers* in front of Romy.

"So I was . . . uhhh . . . wondering," he began. "Are you . . . uhhh . . . going to the Sadie Hawkins dance?" he asked. In addition to being a mouth breather, Todd was a big "uhh"-er as well.

My eyes widened. Uh-oh. A few weeks before, Beatrice had said that a few times she had seen Todd staring at me, all creepy-like. Now he was talking about the dance? Did this mean he liked me? Not to be mean or anything, but I did *not* want him liking me. Frankly, I didn't want any of the boys in our class

127

liking me. I turned around and cleared my throat. "Um, Todd, the whole thing about this kind of dance is that the girls have to ask the boys," I explained nervously. "So technically, you're not allowed to ask me."

He looked at me like I was nuts. "Uhhh, you thought I was going to ask you to the dance?!" he asked. Loudly. Which made pretty much everyone on our side of the room turn around to see who he was talking about. That was another semi-annoying thing about Todd—when he got overexcited, he was almost as loud as Alice. And he didn't even have the excuse that he was deaf in one ear like she did.

I turned as red as my Converses. "Well, I mean, when you said—" I sputtered.

Todd snorted. And not one of those quick snorts I sometimes did when something was semi-funny, but a very long, very loud one. Which, of course, made more people look over. "Uhh, I was just making conversation."

"Oh," I replied, my shoulders reaching up to my ears as I got even more embarrassed.

"Don't take this the wrong way, Lucy—I mean, you're nice and all—but you're not my type," he announced in his loud voice, as I went from red to as purple as the bell-sleeved minidress I had on. "Plus, Denise Milchowski already asked me to go," he added.

Seeing that they were both in the gaming club, that made sense, but still—was *everyone* going to the dance except for me? I saw Ashley tap Noah on the shoulder, and I whipped around and handed Todd the beaker. "Here—hold this!" I ordered as I zoomed across the room so I wouldn't miss what happened next.

"Lucy, what are you doing?" Mr. Eagle Eye asked.

"Oh. I, ah"—I crouched down on the floor—"dropped my pen," I said. Ew. You'd think the floors in such a fancy school would be clean, but it turned out they were disgusting.

"But your lab table is all the way across the room," he said, confused.

"It's one of those pens that roll really fast and really far," I yelled from underneath the table.

"So, Noah, I was wondering—" I heard Ashley say.

I popped my head up from underneath the table.

"Hey, Noah," I said. "Did you know that hanging out with Ashley is a great way to spend an evening?" I asked.

She gave me a weird look. "How would you know?"

"I mean, it's not like you and I have ever actually hung out or anything," I replied, "or, ah, ever even really *talked*, but I can just tell that if we did, it would be great. Because, see, I'm ... a little bit psychic." Now it wasn't just her and Noah who were looking at me weird—it was the four kids at the lab table next to them. Which is why I squatted down on the floor again and started to look for my imaginary pen.

"So you know this Sadie Hawkins dance that's coming up..." I heard Ashley say nervously.

"Yeah. I know about it," came Noah's muffled reply.

I popped up again. "Sorry for interrupting again, but you know what I was just thinking?" I asked. "I was thinking that if I were going to that dance—not that I am, but if I were—I bet you'd be a really good person to go with, Ashley."

I had started to attract a crowd, including Beatrice—who, because she knew about the letters, understood what I was trying to do. And the way she kept shaking her head like she had water in her ears made me think that maybe she didn't think it was a good idea.

I turned to Ashley, who not only looked confused, but also like if I didn't let her get out what she needed to say, she was going to burst. Or get her period right then because of all the stress and embarrassment. Which, according to my log, she had not gotten yet. And if she did, it would make it so that I was that much closer to being one of the only girls in the grade who hadn't gotten it. "Ashley, not only do I think you'd be a good person to go to the dance with," I said, "but even if I couldn't dance because, I don't know . . . I had a *broken leg* or something, I *still* think you'd be a good person to go with. On account of the fact that you're so easy to talk to." I gave a huge gasp. "Oh wow—look at that—Noah, *you* have a broken leg! I completely forgot! Pretty weird that I just said that, huh?"

"Oh boy," I heard Beatrice say.

He shrugged. "I guess."

"Like.... almost ... *fate* kind of weird, right?" I asked.

"Oh no," Beatrice said.

"Lucy Parker, I'd appreciate it if—" Mr. Eagle Eye started to say.

"Lucy *B.* Parker," I corrected him.

"Lucy *B.* Parker, I'd appreciate it if you went back to your lab table now," he said. "I'm sure Todd would like your help."

"Yeah," Todd agreed. With my super-sensitive ears I could hear him mouth breathing all the way across the room.

"Okay, but I just—"

"*Now*, Lucy," Mr. Eagle Eye barked. For the most part, he was really mellow. Like to the point where sometimes when we were taking a quiz and I looked up at him, I could swear he was dozing off even though he'd quickly wake himself up, like Alan did when he fell asleep at the movies. But when he got all barky like he was at that moment? Watch out. There were no "supers" or "wonderfuls" when he was like that.

"Okay, okay," I said, making my way back to my

table. Very slowly. Stopping every few seconds and turning around to see if Ashley had gotten up the courage to follow my advice and ask him until Mr. Eagle Eye barked "Lucy!" even louder and in more of an *I-mean-business* tone than before. Unfortunately, when I got back to my table, Todd decided it was important for him to tell me every single thing that happened in the latest episode of *Monster High*, so I couldn't overlisten to Ashley and Noah with my super-sensitive ears. But when Ashley ran past me into the hall all sniffly, I realized that things probably hadn't gone so well.

"Lucy B. Parker, where do you think you're going?" Mr. Eagle Eye demanded as I started to follow her. You couldn't really blame the guy for sounding all mad, seeing as how he was missing his midmorning nap.

"To the bathroom," I replied. I'd burst into tears during school hours enough times to know that's where I'd be able to find Ashley. "I'm having a . . . *female issue*," I whispered loudly. He turned all red and said, "Fine. Go," rather than putting me through the third degree as to why I couldn't wait five more minutes until lunchtime.

"Ashley?" I called out as I walked into the girls' room down the hall. For heavy-duty, hunkering-down-type crying, I preferred the one near the cafeteria because of its roomy handicapped stall, but when you were having a real meltdown, sometimes you just had to suck it up—in this case, literally, because of the gross smell—and hide out in this one.

The only answer was sniffling coming from the middle stall. I walked up to it. "Ashley, I know you're in there," I said.

"How do you know?" she sniffled.

I pointed at the ground. "Because I can see your lavender Uggs." While I wasn't an Uggs fan (too sweaty), I *was* a purple fan, which is why I made mental notes of who wore the color in what form. "By the way, I keep meaning to tell you I really like them."

"Thanks," she sniffled.

I reached into my back pocket and took out some tissues. They were a bit wrinkled, but because they were the Cold Care tissues with aloe and vitamin E, they were super-soft. Not only that, but they were warm because I had been sitting on them, which kind of made my butt like the towel warmer in Shutters on the Beach, the fancy hotel that Laurel and I stayed in when we went to L.A. "Want a tissue?" I asked. "They're Cold Cares."

"Cold Cares are the best," she sniffled as she put her hand underneath the stall.

"I know," I said, handing them to her. Maybe I should try to get to know Ashley better. Anyone who knew their tissues was worth at least one trip to

Billy's Bakery together. "So are you okay?" I asked. "I mean, from the way you ran out of the room and the fact that you're crying, I'm guessing the answer is no," I said, "so I wanted to see if you wanted to talk about it. Even though we're not really friends. And, uh, I have no experience asking boys to dances."

She opened the door a crack. "How do you know I asked someone to the dance?" she demanded.

I shrugged. "I don't. I mean, I just had this psychic hunch that that's what happened," I lied. Well, not exactly lied. I mean, I hadn't actually heard her say the words *Noah, would you like to go to the Sadie Hawkins dance with me?*" so I kind of *was* going on psychic ability at that moment. "But, ah, *did* you ask someone to the dance?"

Not a good question to ask unless you want to watch someone burst into tears, complete with a running nose. "*Yessss!*" she bawled.

"And what did he say?" I asked hopefully. It was probably pushing it to think that Noah had said yes and Ashley was just having some sort of weird opposite-like reaction, like how sometimes after announcing "Boy, I'm completely stuffed!" after chowing down on Rose's delicious fried plantains, I then ate more of them.

"He said *nooooooo!*" she bawled ever louder.

Okay, so much for that theory.

"You know the 'Ask Annie' advice column in the school newspaper?" she hiccuped.

I pretended to think really hard. "Hmm . . . I *think* I may have seen it at some point."

"Well, I wrote to her and she said that it was okay to ask someone to the dance who couldn't dance because of a broken leg," she sniffled, "because as long as I asked him questions about him, we wouldn't run out of conversation."

I nodded. "Huh. That sounds like good advice," I said. "This Annie person sounds smart."

"And then, because this person who had a broken leg spent the entire science period saying things like, 'Boy, I sure would like to go to the Sadie Hawkins dance' and 'Even though I can't dance, I sure would like to go to the Sadie Hawkins dance and sit on the bleachers and talk about dancing—like the dancers in that *America's Worst Dancers* show, which, even though I don't really watch, I hear is really good—'"

Uh-oh. I didn't like where this was going. That being said, it was nice to see that not only had Noah taken my advice about how to let Romy know he was interested, but also about not lying about having seen the show.

"—I thought that was a good sign that he'd say yes if I asked him," she continued. "I mean, wouldn't you think that was a good sign if you were in my shoes?"

I shrugged. "Yeah, I guess." Unless someone, like me, had given him advice to say that so someone *else*, like Romy, would ask him to the dance.

"So I asked him. And he said no!" she wailed, busting out into a whole new slew of tears.

"I'm sorry, Ashley," I said, patting her arm and trying to stay clear of anything that might be dripping out of her nose. "Hey, can I give you some advice?"

She looked at me like I had just said, "Hey, you want to see me burst into flames right now?" "More advice?" she said bitterly. "I don't think so. In fact, I think I'm going to send a petition around to see about getting Annie fired. My dumb brother could do better than her in that job, and he's only eight."

"Well, everyone's allowed an off day here and there," I said nervously. This wasn't good. What if the entire class revolted against Annie, like the Russian peasants did in 1905 (my brain may not have worked good for math-like stuff, but for some reason history facts stuck in it like Jolly Ranchers did to my molars), and there was an uprising, complete with ANNIE MUST GO! posters and marches? That would be beyond embarrassing. "But let's not talk about Annie anymore," I said. "Plus, this is really good advice," I said. "Pete, my doorman, gave it to me, and he's pretty much the smartest person I know, even if he didn't go to college. And everyone knows doorman advice is the best advice around."

"We don't have a doorman," she sniffled. "We live in a loft in Tribeca."

"Well, trust me—it is," I replied. "So what Pete is always saying to me is that as long as you're yourself, you're always going to end up meeting the people you need to meet," I said. "You know, the ones who will get you and your Ashleyness."

"My Ashleyness?"

"Yeah. My mom's the one who came up with that term. You know, all the stuff that makes you . . . Ashley," I explained. "And if for some reason this boy with a broken leg doesn't want to spend an evening on the bleachers talking to you, finding out more about your Ashleyness, then that just means that you're supposed to be hanging out with someone else that night who will get you more."

"Like who?" she asked.

I shrugged. "I don't know . . . maybe . . . me?" I suggested. "I mean, I'm not going to the dance."

"Really? You're not? How come?"

"I hurt my ankle a few weeks ago, and it's still kind of sore, so I feel like I should rest it. You know, so it'll be better for gym." Okay, that was a total lie. I barely ever took part in gym, thanks to the forged

"Please-excuse-Lucy-from-gym-class-as-she-is-menstruating" note that Marissa had written for me last year that I had luckily photocopied so I could use it in New York, too.

"But you're class president."

"That's another reason why I don't think I should go," I replied. If I had known I was going to get so much grief about the dance because of the president thing, I never would've run for office. "So that I don't, you know, take attention away from everyone else because I'm president. Maybe we could go to the movies or something that night." I'd just TiVo the *Hoarders* marathon.

It was nice to see her smile. "Really?"

I nodded. It felt good to ask Ashley if she wanted to hang out. She was on the quiet side, and didn't have too many friends, which was something I knew about. Not the quiet part, but the not-so-many-friends part.

"Okay," she said.

I smiled back. "Cool."

It was the least I could do for giving her advice that didn't work out. Even if there was nothing in the column that said that the advice had to work. In fact, if I continued with it, I was going to ask Dr. Rem-Wall if she could put something in that said *Note to readers: Annie does not and cannot promise your life will work out even if you take her advice.* "I guess I'll go to lunch now," I said as I reached into my other pocket and pulled out some more tissues. "Here," I said, handing them to her. "In case you need them for later."

She took them. "Thanks. For everything. I'm still not sure what that Ashleyness thing means, but you're pretty good with this advice stuff."

I smiled. "I'll Facebook you about the movie thing," I said as I walked out.

I spent the rest of the afternoon thinking about the Ashley/Noah thing. During history, I came up with a great idea. An idea so great that it would make it that Ashley wouldn't be able to go to the movies with me. Because she'd be at the dance instead.

"Hey Noah—wait up!" I called as school let out later that day. Because of his cast, he couldn't walk very fast. A good thing for someone like me, who hated anything gym-like, which, as far as I was concerned, walking fast *was*.

"What is it?" he asked suspiciously as I caught up with him.

I shrugged. "Nothing. I just thought it would be nice to walk home together," I panted. "You know, get to know each other."

"But I thought you lived over on Central Park West?" he said as we walked west toward Riverside Drive in the opposite direction from my apartment.

"Oh, I do," I replied. "But sometimes I walk this way. For the exercise." It wasn't a total lie. I mean, maybe I'd find out that I actually *liked* walking for exercise. But probably not. "So I was wondering . . . are you going to the Sadie Hawkins dance?" I blurted out. My original plan was to be all smooth about the whole thing and kind of ease into it—some small talk, some taking my own advice and asking him questions about himself—but then I realized that if I did that, it would (a) make it a very long walk, and (b) I would miss Dr. Maude's show because I had forgotten to TiVo it. And with the way things were going, I couldn't afford to miss a single episode.

He stopped walking. "Are you asking me to the dance, *too*? Is that why you were so weird in science?"

"What? No!" I cried. "I was just . . . taking a poll. And you were the next person on the poll." I had to admit that while I was very impressed with my ability to come up with believable-sounding things on the spot, I was a little nervous about how good I was getting at lying. What if I turned into Stacey Manderson, this girl in the eighth grade who lied so much she was sent away to some special boarding school where there wasn't *one TV* in the entire place? "It's research. For student council."

"Well, I had *wanted* to go, but then I got some really bad advice from that Annie girl in the paper, which screwed it all up. I hope she gets fired," he grumbled. "Maybe I could sue her," he added. Like Cristina, Noah's dad was a lawyer, too.

My eyes widened. Talk about people hating on you. "What happened?" I asked.

"She told me to keep yelling how much I wanted to go in front of the person I wanted to go with."

"She didn't use the word *yelling*," I said.

His eyes narrowed. "How do you know?"

I shrugged. "I read it in the column this morning."

He stopped walking. "But it wasn't *in* the column."

He was right. Because I wasn't as popular as Dr. Maude (yet), what happened was that I answered all the letters and sent back responses, and then depending on how much space was available in the paper that week, a bunch of them got printed. But no matter what, everyone got an answer.

I stopped, too. "Okay, listen. I'm about to tell you something I don't tell a lot of people. And if you repeat it, I'll have to . . ." I tried to think of something that would really scare him. "Well, I'm not exactly sure what I'll have to do, but it won't be good."

"You'll have to lock me in a small cell and let water

drip so that I slowly start to go crazy until I tell you that, yes, okay, I'll spill all the government secrets I know?" he asked excitedly.

"Sure." I shrugged. "Anyway, I don't like to talk about it too much, but the truth is . . ." I sighed. "I'm psychic. And that's how I knew."

"You're not psychic," he scoffed.

"I am, too!" I cried. "And that's how I know that Annie also told you that you should bring up the *America's Worst Dancers* thing only if you actually watched it. Otherwise, you'd be lying, which would give you bad karma."

"She *did* say that!" he exclaimed.

"See? I told you. Look, whether I'm psychic or not doesn't really matter. What matters is that, if you ask me, that sounds like really good advice. I mean, if it were me, I'd totally follow it."

"Then you'd be dumb. Because you want to know what the person who I was asking for advice about did?" he demanded.

I cringed. Actually, I didn't, but I was too far into this thing now to walk away. Plus, my lack-of-direction issues had kicked up, and if I did walk away, chances were it would be in the wrong direction, and then not only would I miss Dr. Maude, but I'd also miss Dr. Dave. "I guess so," I said.

"She said 'Are you deaf in one ear like Alice Mosher?

Because you talk really loud. I think you need to get your hearing checked.' And then she asked someone else right in front of me!"

I cringed. "Oh. That's not good." I brightened. "But, hey, look at it this way—at least you found out right away that Romy's not very nice, rather than having to spend a whole evening with her."

"How'd you know it was Romy?" he demanded.

"Obviously, it's the psychic thing," I replied nervously. "Anyway, not only did you find out she wasn't nice, but now you can go with someone who *is* nice. And lucky for you, I just happen to know someone who would be a great match for you. Because of the psychic thing."

"Who?"

"Ashley."

"Ashley who?"

"Your lab partner."

"The girl with the blonde hair?"

I nodded.

"So *that's* her name. You know, she asked me to the dance in class," he said.

I rolled my eyes. People were always giving me grief for not choosing a local crush (or a long-distance/vacation one, or a celebrity one), but as far as I was concerned, why would I bother when all a crush did was make you miserable? I mean, to spend all your time thinking about someone—even going as far as to write a letter to a famous advice columnist about the person (fine—maybe not *famous*-famous, like known to the world, but famous at the Center for Creative Learning)—only to then find out that not only was that person not thinking *back* about you, but he didn't even know your *name*? That sounded about as fun as having the old woman at Orchard Corset yell at you that if you kept slumping, your boobies were going to end up on your knees when you were her age.

If Dad were there, he'd tell me it wasn't nice to make what he called "sweeping generalizations," which is when you grouped an entire group of people together and said something not so nice about them, such as "All boys are dumb," but in this case, I'm sorry, all boys *were* dumb.

I shrugged. "My psychicness told me that she would be a good person for you to go to the dance with," I said. "Because of how nice she is."

"She is?"

"Oh yeah," I replied. "I mean, I can understand why you might not know that, on account of the fact that she's on the quiet side, and the fact that you don't know her name, even though you do experiments together, but, yes, she's really nice." Boy, I hoped that was true, or else I was making an even bigger mess than I had already. Seeing that the only time I had spent with Ashley had been in the bathroom that afternoon—where I did most of the talking and she did most of the crying—I couldn't be positive about the nice thing. "She's just shy. Which is *another* reason why you should go with her," I added. "I know it might seem hard to believe, but *I'm* shy, too," I admitted.

"You are?"

I nodded. "Yeah. And as a shy person, I'm here to tell you that sometimes we end up missing out on things in life because we're so afraid of people saying no to us shy people that we just don't ask."

Noah looked completely confused. Not that I blamed him. I was starting to confuse myself. "Look, all I'm saying is that if Ashley asked you to the dance," I went on, "you might want to reconsider going with her."

"I don't know . . ." he said, doubtfully. "She seems kind of . . . quiet."

"Well, yeah, but that might not be such a bad thing," I replied. "You know how a lot of people—especially girls—go on and on about themselves and you can't even get a word in edgewise?" I asked. "Well, she doesn't do that. She's a very curious person, so she likes to hear people talk about themselves. In fact, you could probably talk about yourself all night and she wouldn't mind."

"Huh. That sounds like it could be cool," he replied. He nodded. "Okay. I guess now that Romy's not going to ask me, maybe I could go with—what's her name again?" he asked.

Whether it was a "gross generalization" or not, I was going to say it again: boys were dumb. "It's Ashley," I replied.

He nodded. "Yeah. Her. I'll tell her tomorrow in class."

I so deserved some huge medal for saving this one. As we got to Broadway, I stopped. "I'm going to turn here and go home now," I said. Now that I had kind-of-sort-of saved the day I wanted to get out of there as soon as possible so I wouldn't end up getting myself in more trouble.

"Okay. See you tomorrow," he said. "And thanks for the advice."

"Anytime," I replied.

While walking down Broadway and turning onto Seventy-second Street so I could stop at Buttercup Bakery (if saving the day wasn't a good excuse for a cupcake, I didn't know what was), I thought about adding "matchmaker" to my list of hobbies, if just one item on the list (advice giving) could be considered "a list." Sure, maybe my hobbies weren't the regular ones that kids my age had, but at least they had to do with *helping* people. Kind of like if I had volunteered to read to people at a nursing home, which is something that

Alice's mother made her do after she got grounded for texting during church. Well, she did it until the old people—even the ones who were almost deaf and had to wear hearing aids—complained that her loud talking was hurting their ears and the woman who ran the place fired her.

As I paid for my red velvet cupcake (not as good as the ones at Billy's Bakery downtown, but a billion times better than the ones at Crumbs), my phone buzzed with a text. *I asked Chris to the dance—and he said yes!* Beatrice had written. *I think the being nice part really helped* ☺. I smiled. I was happy for her. Some of my advice may have backfired, but some of it did work out.

But that meant all my friends were going, and I wasn't.

All because I couldn't seem to take my—or anyone else's—advice and just get up the guts to (a) tell my BFF I had an official crush on her brother, and then (b) ask him to a dance.

chapter 7

Dear Dr. Maude,

I just wanted to let you know that in case you were worried about me because of my last e-mail (if you never bothered to look at it, it was the one that said "Dear Dr. Maude, Just in case you were wondering, this advice thing has gotten completely out of control. Like so out of control that I can't even go into it at the moment. Yours truly, Lucy B. Parker), I'm okay. At least PHYSICALLY.

Nonphysically, things are not so good. As you know, there are a lot of things I'm not so good at. Like things that you need coordination for. Or a good singing voice. Or an empty stomach. So when I found out I actually had some talent when it came to this advice thing, I got excited. Especially the other day when Alan told me he was proud of me. But now I have to admit I'm not so excited about it. I don't know if you've ever had this experience, but sometimes the whole advice thing blows up in your face, and then you have to work really, really hard to try and fix things. Actually, now that I think about it, you HAVE had the blowing-up-in-your-face experience—when that crazy woman from Alaska managed to get past the security guards and came on stage and started screaming about how you had ruined her marriage because you had told her husband that anyone who had more than three cats was officially crazy. And then she threw a bucket of red paint on you. And now that I think about it, there's something on your website that says that you refuse to discuss that incident and will end all interviews if anyone dares to bring it up. So you can forget I mentioned it.

I was able to help some kids at school who had asked for advice about the dance, but I still haven't come up with a solution as to what to do about the fact that my parents both took my advice and have now planned two different vacations. I think I'd like to take a break from the advice business for a while and just go back to being an average girl who has no hobbies and probably won't get into college. (Although, according to Pete, there's a lid for every pot. Usually, he says that when talking about people finding someone to marry, but he says it works with colleges, too.)

I'd ask for some advice about how to fix things, but at this point I'm not sure even you can help me.

yours truly,
LUCY B. PARKER

There may not have been any amount of advice that could help me—especially as it got closer to Mom and Alan's anniversary, and I still hadn't figured out a way to fix things—but because I still had my job, I had to give advice to other people. It was weird how, while I couldn't help myself, I was great when it came to other people.

Just that morning a letter had been printed where I—I mean, *Annie*—had been asked what the proper name was for the stepbrother of your stepsister of your stepbrother. Technically, the person who wrote it wasn't asking for advice, but I answered it anyway because I thought it was both (a) interesting and (b) important, due to the fact that so many kids in our school had blended families. It took me a while, but I finally settled on "tribrother," because "tri" means three and this person was three people removed.

At lunch, as I was walking through the cafeteria to my table in Alaska, I heard Sarah Langdon say to Stacy Woo, "My tribrother's going to be spending Thanksgiving with his trimother and bifather." ("Bi" means two removed, like bicycle, which has two wheels, instead of a tricycle, which has three.)

That made me feel good at school, but by the time I got home I was back to not really feeling it. "Why am I even bothering to do this?" I asked Laurel. I sat on the couch with my laptop logging on to my AskAnnie4Advice@ gmail.com account while she practiced some tai chi moves from a book. She was taking lessons, though her first class wasn't for two months because she was too busy with the TV show and all her other Regular Girl activities to fit it in before then. I kept trying to tell her that the CPR class, while a good thing to do, wasn't exactly something that most Regular Girls did, but she was really enjoying it. She had been on me to take CPR with her, but once I reminded her about my coordination problem, she agreed that maybe we should find some other non-lifesaving Regular Girl activity to do together (coordination problems + trying to save someone's life = might end up seriously hurting if not killing them). I said that if there was a cupcake-making class, I'd be interested in that one, but so far we hadn't found one.

"Don't people realize that even if you give them the best advice in the world, at the end of the day, life is just one big problem after that next?" I asked. "Oh wait. That's just *my* life."

"Oh, come on, Lucy," Laurel said as she balanced on her right leg while crouching down and sweeping her arms back and forth as if she was cleaning a window. How did people do that balancing thing without falling flat on their faces? And how was she so good at it her first time ever doing it? "It's not that bad. So you don't have the guts to tell Beatrice you have a crush on Blair and then ask him to the dance. Or to ruin Dad and Rebecca's one-year anniversary by telling them that the advice you gave each of them made it so that everything got screwed up—"

I looked at her. "Okay, you're not helping."

"Wait. I'm not done! What I was going to say was that I probably wouldn't have the guts to do those things, either."

"But what about that whole 'heroes are heroes because they do things even when they're afraid' speech you gave me last month when I was running for president?" I asked.

"Huh. I forgot about that."

As my e-mail account loaded, I paled. "Three hundred twenty-six messages?!" I yelped.

Laurel hopped over—gracefully. "Whoops. I guess that interview I did for youngmademoiselle.com ran already. I knew there was something I forgot to mention to you."

"What do you mean?"

"Well, when the writer asked me what great new things I had come across lately, I told her there was this awesome advice column called 'Ask Annie,' and then I may have, I don't know, mentioned the e-mail address?" she said.

"Laurel, it's an advice column for my school paper!" I said. "Not for"—I scrolled through the e-mails—"kids in *Athens, Greece* or"—I scrolled some more—"*St. Petersburg, Russia!*"

"But you're so good at this stuff!" she cried. "People around the world should be able to benefit from it! Plus, if I were your publicist, I'd tell you that it's totally un-PC to discriminate against people from other countries."

"Look, you know I love people from other countries. And food—I'm a huge fan of *food* from other countries, like falafel and pizza—but if I hand these in to be printed in the column, they're going to know that these kids don't go to the Center," I said.

"You don't know that for sure," Laurel said. "There are many problems that kids go through that are completely universal."

I read through some of the e-mails. "Oh yeah? How about this one?" I asked. "*Dear Annie, Yesterday, when I went out to the shed behind our cabin to feed our goats, there was one missing. I cannot say for sure, but I think that my neighbor is responsible for this thievery, especially because he is known as being the meanest boy in my village. My grandmother would like to put a spell on him, but I think that that is not fair until we discover if he is indeed the culprit. Do you agree with this plan of action? I would be most grateful for your advice. Thank you, Concerned in Congo.*'" I looked up. "Isn't Congo in Africa?" I asked.

Laurel nodded.

"Wow. Maybe I'm *not* completely hopeless at geography like I thought," I said, impressed.

"Wow. Who knew I had fans who owned *goats*?" said Laurel, impressed.

"If this ran in the paper, people would get really suspicious," I said. "Last time I checked, there weren't a lot of goats running around on the Upper West Side." There was, however, this guy who walked down Broadway with a cat on his head and would let you take a picture of it for a dollar. Or yell at you really loud and embarrass you in front of everyone if he caught you trying to take one without his realizing it. (Unfortunately, I had firsthand experience with that second part.)

Laurel walked over to me and glanced over my shoulder at the computer screen. "Okay, so maybe the universal things are more like pimples and B.O.," she said. She pointed to an e-mail that said "Anxious on Amsterdam Ave" in the subject line. "Here—read that one. At least it takes place in Manhattan."

Unless there was an Amsterdam Avenue in, say, *Iran* or somewhere like that. I clicked it open.

I opened it. "*Dear Annie*," I read, "*You know this Sadie Hawkins dance that's coming up? (Of course you do—because you've already answered like a million questions about it.) Well, I'd really like to go, and I know who I want to go with, but I have a really big problem: I'm too afraid to do it because I'm afraid he's going to say no and then I'd feel really stupid. I don't think it's a big deal if other people get rejected, but when it comes to me, I just feel way too scared, so I'd rather not take the risk. And I think it would be really sad if I didn't go because I have a dress picked out and everything. Signed, Anxious on Amsterdam Ave.*"

I sighed. There were a lot of reasons I'd be glad when the dance was finally over, but the main one was that Annie could move on to different topics. Like, say, what to do when your cat hated you and your parents refused to get you a new kitten. Miss Piggy glared at me from her perch near Laurel.

"'Dear Anxious,'" I typed. "'Okay, maybe he'll say no, and if he does, maybe you'll feel stupid for like two seconds—probably ten minutes at the most—but here's the thing: If you don't ask, you'll never know what his answer will be! And if you don't know what his answer is, you won't know if you should bother to shave your legs so they're not all gross and hairy the day of the dance when you wear the dress. (I guess you could just wear the dress anyway, at home, in your room, and it wouldn't matter if your legs were hairy because no one else would be seeing them except for your cat, who you would have locked in there because, even though she's mean to you, you still keep hoping she'll start being nice to you one day, but that's a whole other subject.)

"'Everyone gets scared and everyone is scared of rejection (okay, maybe not a certain girl in our school with the initials C.P., but that, too, is a whole other subject), but recently a very smart person told me that a hero is someone who is scared but doesn't let that stop them from doing what they're scared of doing. So my advice to you would be to just take a deep breath, maybe say a little prayer to whoever it is that you pray to when you're about to do something scary (it doesn't have to be God, or Buddha—it can just be a doorknob or your favorite pair of sneakers), and then just do it.

"'If he says yes, great; if not, then, oh well. Either way, then you can take all that time that you've been spending

thinking about it and put it toward something more
interesting . . . like, say, how to get your parents to let you
adopt a kitten. Good luck! Annie.'"

I looked at Laurel. "How does that sound?"

She nodded. "Awesome. But you know what this means, don't you?"

"That someone who works in TV might see this and offer me my own talk show?"

She shook her head. "Nope. That you're going to have to ask Blair to the dance."

"What?! Why?"

She shrugged. "Because you wouldn't be a very good advice columnist if you didn't take your own advice."

Again with the you-need-to-take-your-own-advice thing! My eyes narrowed. "That's not fair."

"It's not like anyone would find out that you're not taking your own advice, but *you'd* know."

"Okay, that's really not fair!" I cried. Recently, I'd started feeling guilty about a lot of things, even though I had no reason to feel guilty about them. Beatrice called it a "Jewish guilt complex," and said that it had probably developed since I'd moved to New York and been around a lot more Jewish people than I had been in Northampton. And knowing you weren't taking your own advice would definitely bring on a lot of guilt.

Laurel shrugged again and went back to perfectly balancing on her other leg. "But I wouldn't worry about it too much," she said. "Like I said, no one will know that while you're giving people great advice about being brave, you won't ask the boy you want to ask to the dance." She patted my arm. "It's okay. I understand. It's fine."

I sighed. No it wasn't.

It wasn't fine at all.

chapter 8

Dear Dr. Maude,

Before I get to the real reason that I'm writing to you, I keep meaning to ask you whether you have an older sister or a frister, and if so, if she was the kind of sister/frister who, when you were young, tried to push you into things using reverse psychology like mine does to me. And if so, because she was an actress, she was able to do it in such a way that you didn't realize until way after that it was reverse psychology.

Because that's what Laurel did to me yesterday, and now I have this huge problem (as if I need another one). Not only that, but I'm pretty sure that this e-mail I got from "Anxious on Amsterdam Ave" was actually written by her even though we live on Central Park West rather than Amsterdam.

Okay, so this is my question: Have you ever been in a situation where you've given someone advice, but then when you found yourself in the SAME EXACT situation they were in, you weren't willing to do the very thing that you had told that person they should do, even though it was obviously awesome advice because it came from you? (BTW, if the answer is yes, you don't have to worry about me telling anyone. I won't. Because if the situations were reversed, I wouldn't want people knowing I was a hypocrite. Which, I'm sure you know, is kind of like being a liar, but not exactly.)

That's the situation I'm in right now—I don't want to take my own advice. Because even though I told Anxious on Amsterdam that she should just ask the boy she likes, I don't think that I can do that with Blair.

But I also don't want to be a hypocrite.

So as you can see, I'm what Alan would call "in between a rock and a hard place," even though there aren't any rocks in my room at the moment, and where I actually am is in between a blanket and a sheet.

I know I've said at different times that I really, really need advice, but this time I really DO need advice. And fast.

Thanks.

yours truly,
LUCY B. PARKER

The good news about my newest problem was that it took my mind off my old problems. Like, say, how to clean up the mess I had made with my advice to Mom and Alan about their anniversary weekend. At least for a few minutes.

"Hi Lucyloo!" Alan cried as he stumbled into the apartment with a bunch of bags from Paragon Sporting Goods.

"Hi," I replied mopily. Having just cured my dad of calling me Monkey in public, I wasn't thrilled about another dumb nickname, but the fact that Alan had gone to all the trouble to come up with one meant a lot to me. Especially because once I got out of the advice business, he'd probably be disappointed in me and take it away. I pointed at the bag. "What's that?"

"Just some things I thought might come in handy during our weekend in Vermont," he replied. He pulled out a pair of snowshoes. "I figured snowshoeing could be fun. A lot less dangerous than downhill skiing. Or even cross-country skiing."

"But there's no snow on the ground," I replied, confused.

He pulled out two tennis racquets. "That's why I brought these!" He reached into another bag. "And I found a great travel backgammon board. For when we get sick of all that fresh country air." He walked over and gave me a big hug. "Lucy, I can't thank you enough for coming up with such a fantastic idea."

"It wasn't *that* great of an idea," I replied.

He ruffled my hair. "You're so modest. That's good. College admissions people like that."

"I was thinking . . . maybe you should tell Mom about all this," I said nervously. "Just in case, you know, she doesn't *want* to go to Vermont—"

"And ruin the surprise? No way!" He picked up the bags. "Now I'm going to go hide these in my office so she doesn't find them."

As he walked away, I sighed. The fact that I couldn't get up the guts to tell Alan what a mess I'd made kind of made me a hypocrite as well.

I'm not a big pray-er, even though THAT probably made me a hypocrite, too, seeing that I had told Anxious to pray to a doorknob and ask for courage before she asked the boy to the dance. But before I went to sleep that night, because Dr. Maude still hadn't written me back (I practically drained the battery on my iTouch checking all during dinner, until Mom caught me and said she'd take it away from me for good unless I stopped), I decided to give it a try. Not praying-for-courage-to-ask-Blair-to-the-dance, but just praying-to-figure-out-what-the-heck-I-should-do. I even decided to stand in front of the doorknob in order to take care of the hypocrite issue.

"Hi . . . Go—" I was about to say God, but then I decided that if there was an actual person named God, He or She might feel really insulted to be grouped in with things like doorknobs.

"Hi, Bud—" I was going to say Buddha, until I decided that even though from everything Mom and Dad had told me about the guy, he was a lot more easygoing and laid back than God, even someone like that might be offended by the doorknob thing. I sighed. This praying thing was tricky.

"Hi . . . Doorknob," I finally landed on. Because whatever I was praying to was really smart, it would know that I really meant Him or Her. "My name is Lucy B. Parker and . . . wait, hold on a sec," I said as I kneeled down so I was on my knees like the praying people you saw in movies. "Okay. That's better. Anyway, as I was saying, I'm not sure if You remember me on account of the fact that we don't talk all that often, but I hope You won't hold that against me and instead help me out here because I really really really need it."

I stopped for a second to see if there was any answer, even if it was just a book falling off my bookshelf, which is also something that happened in movies when people were talking to God or ghosts, but nothing happened. Other than me burping, which I really hoped He/She knew wasn't because I was being disrespectful but because we had had couscous for dinner, which, for some reason, always made me burp afterward.

"Sorry about that. So listen, it's kind of a long story, so I won't go into all of it right now, plus, because You're You, You probably already know what this is about because I'm pretty sure You're psychic and can therefore read my mind. So, if that's the case, You know what I'm talking about here is needing a sign as to whether I should take my own advice and tell Beatrice I kind-of-sort-of may like her brother and then ask him to the Sadie Hawkins dance."

I got quiet again in case the sign came at that moment—like, say, in the form of Miss Piggy upchucking a hairball—but all she did was stare at me from the corner with what I swear was a "You are sooo weird" expression on her face. (She hated me so much that she wouldn't even lie on my bed unless I physically held her down there. But Laurel's bed? She jumped right up there and wouldn't get down even when you said, "Come on, Miss Piggy, it's dinnertime.")

"Okay, well, I guess the sign will come later then," I continued. "But if You could just really make it clear as to whether the answer is *yes*, I should ask him, or *no*, I should not, I'd appreciate that. So I'm going to stand up now, if that's okay, because this kneeling thing is really uncomfortable. Plus, I have to pee." I stood up. "I hope You have a good night, wherever You are. Bye. Oh, and thank You very much in advance. Yours truly, Lucy B. Parker."

Huh. That wasn't half as scary as I thought it would be. In fact, maybe if this all worked out, I'd do this praying thing on a regular basis.

Unfortunately, by the time I left for school the next morning, no signs had shown up. No weird dreams or rattling windows while I slept. That kind of thing happened a lot when we lived in Northampton because our house was over a hundred years old, which meant that things were always rattling or creaking or breaking, but in New York, everything was new, because Alan had had the apartment redone a year before we moved there. No hairballs when I woke up. I had locked Miss Piggy in my room that night for that very reason. No words spelled out with my cereal the next morning.

And if a sign had shown up as I was walking to school with Beatrice, it's not like I would've noticed, because that's when the Question Incident happened, and if I had learned anything over the last year, it was that when Incidents with Capital I's were happening, everything else kind of fell to the side because they were so dramatic.

Our walk started off normal. Like always, I was late (this time it was because I kept running back to my bathroom to see if a sign had appeared on the mirror), which, like always, made Beatrice all annoyed. And like always, we stopped at Hakim's cart for doughnuts. But soon after that, as I was brushing off the powdered sugar that I always managed to get all over my sweater, things changed.

"Lucy, there's something I need to ask you," Beatrice said as she marched down Broadway while I ran to keep up with her. (People who had lived in Manhattan their whole lives tended to walk really, really fast.)

"What?" I panted.

She stopped and turned to me. "And I really need you to tell me the truth."

Stopping short like that almost made me trip, but I managed to keep upright. "Okay, yes, I *was* praying last night," I admitted. "It's not like it's that big a deal. Lots of people do it!"

She looked confused. "Huh?"

"Nothing. Never mind. Of course I'm going to tell you the truth—you're my BFF. That would be like number one in our official BFF handbook. What is it that you want to know?" I asked nervously as I applied some Watermelon Lip Smacker. When people started conversations with "And I really need you to tell me the truth," it usually wasn't followed with questions like "Where'd you get that barrette?"

"Okay. What I need to know is . . . do you have a crush on Blair?"

Uh-oh. If I threw up at that moment, the sight of cereal mixed with a doughnut was not going to be pretty. "Huh?" I asked nervously. I banged on my left ear. "I think my ear is all clogged up. I didn't hear what you just said," I replied, trying to buy some time. I looked up at the sky. "If this is Your idea of a sign, it's really not fair," I whispered.

"What?"

"Nothing," I said. "Can you please repeat the question?"

"I said . . . do you have a crush on Blair?"

"Blair who?"

"Lucy!"

"What?! I just want to make sure I answer your question correctly. I mean, there are a lot of Blairs in the world. There's, you know, your brother Blair, and there's, um . . ." Unfortunately, I couldn't think of any others at the moment. Probably because I didn't know any.

Beatrice put her hand on her right hip and jutted her chin forward, which was code for, Now I'm starting to get really mad. Mom's way of saying it was crossing her arms in front of her chest and tapping her left foot. Alan's way of saying it was to call an Emergency Family Meeting and put "Reason Why I Am Disappointed" as the first thing on the agenda.

I looked up at the sky again. "Fine. But I'm going to say it again—NOT FAIR," I mumbled.

"Lucy, *what* are you doing?"

I sighed. I guess if I really wanted to, I could lie and say no. And then later on, if the lie was ever discovered, say that the reason I did it was because right before it came out of my mouth, I had been body snatched with the little girl who was screaming as her nanny dragged her down the street because she looked like the kind of kid who lied on a regular basis. Which, as I thought about it, would be another lie, and that wasn't a good thing. Plus if I did that, then (a) I'd screw up my karma, and (b) God or who/whatever was out there would probably get mad because He/She/It had gone to the trouble of giving me a very clear sign as to what I was supposed to do (i.e., tell Beatrice about the crush).

"Just so I'm completely clear, what you're asking is whether I have a crush on your brother Blair?" I asked. Beatrice hated to be late—even to places like school—and I hoped that if I kept stalling, she'd just give up and start marching down the street again.

"Yes. That's what I'm asking."

I didn't dare mop my forehead with my sleeve on account of the fact that (a) sweating is a common sign that a person is nervous or embarrassed, and (b) Beatrice was the one who had told me that. "Okay. Well, if that's what you're asking," I said, as I felt a drop of sweat plop down onto my upper lip, "then I guess I have to tell the truth and say that . . . no, I do not have a crush on your brother Blair."

Her eyes narrowed. "You don't?"

I sighed. "Well, not, you know, *officially*. Because if it were *official*, I would have put it in the log. And I haven't. Yet. But now that we've had this conversation . . . I may think about doing so." Phew. As the words left my mouth, my knees buckled a little. Who knew it felt so good to tell the truth? Even if it meant she'd probably no longer want to be my friend, let alone my best friend. "And just so you know, a large part of why I recently decided that I had an unofficial crush on him is because you're always on me about choosing a local crush, and because we live in the same building, you can't get much more local than that."

As I babbled and blurted and blovershared, Beatrice just stood there with a look of horror on her face. When I finally bit my tongue to shut myself up, I waited for her to let out some long giant scream or go running down the street like the main character did in the movie *Mall Food Court Massacre* that Laurel and I had watched the other night on cable. (She had been offered the lead and had luckily turned it down because it was REALLY bad.) But all she did was scratch the side of her nose.

"Well, it was fun being BFFs while it lasted," I went

on. "If you want, I'll give you Malia as your new one, and I'll just stick with Laurel. I don't mind not having one at school."

"What are you talking about?" she asked, confused. "Why would I want a new BFF?"

I shrugged. "Because you're always going on about how annoying Blair is. And stupid. And gross. And how any girl who had a crush on him was in need of serious mental help."

She shrugged. "Well, yeah, he is all of those things. And I have to say, I have no idea why when there's nine billion boys in the world, you'd pick him as your official local crush—"

"But I just told you he's not my *official* local crush," I corrected. "It's not in the log yet. There's a big difference."

"Fine. Whatever. But if it's between you liking him and having you as my best friend, of course I'm not going to stop it."

"You're not?" I asked, surprised.

She shook her head.

I was so relieved I was sure it was bringing on my period that very second. "But how'd you know?" I asked.

She shrugged. "I don't know. I just did."

That was one of the cool things about being BFFs with someone—the whole mind-reading thing, like how you could finish each other's sentences, or psychically know who they had crushes on. Actually, that part wasn't so good, but the finishing-the-sentences part was.

"I guess it's the way, when we're hanging out in my apartment, you always ask where he is, and when he's coming back," she continued. "Or how, when he's home, you end up going to the bathroom a bunch of times because it means you have to walk past his bedroom to get there."

I did? Whoops.

"Or how, when I bring his name up, your face turns red—kind of like it is now—and when I mentioned that girl Lori Spellman who he danced with at his bar mitzvah last year, you kept asking me all these questions about her. Or how—"

I felt like my cheeks were going to burst into flames any moment. "Okay. You can stop now," I interrupted. "I get why you may have possibly thought that I sort-of-kind-of been a little interested in him. So . . . you're not mad at me?" I asked. "For keeping it a secret?"

"No. I mean, if it were me, I'd be embarrassed to admit it, too," she replied. "But I was thinking . . . seeing that he's your official local crush—"

"Beatrice!"

"Okay, fine—*un*official official crush. That you should probably ask him to the dance."

I looked up at the sky again. "Wait a minute—*another* sign?" I shouted.

"*Why* do you keep doing that?" Beatrice demanded.

I ignored her question. "Really? You think I should ask him to the dance?"

"Yeah. Not because I want him there—because obviously, I don't—and if he did anything to embarrass me, I'd make sure my moms punished him for it, but it would be weird to not have you there. Sure, Malia and Alice will be there, but you're my best friend. It just wouldn't be the same without you."

I smiled.

"And because you won't just ask Mark Bialy—"

The smile faded. "I keep telling you, Mark Bialy smells gross. And he spits when he talks."

She shrugged. "Well, it's not like you can afford to be all picky when the dance is only days away. So as I was saying, because you won't ask him, you should probably just ask my brother. Even if he is stupid. And an embarrassment to society."

"But what if he says no?" I asked.

"Then you can watch that thing on hoarders you want to watch. But at least you'll know you had the courage to at least ask."

That sounded exactly like the advice I had given Anxious on Amsterdam. I took a deep breath. "Okay, fine. I'll do it," I agreed.

What was the worst thing that could happen?

Other than his saying no.

I guess it would be ...

His saying yes.

Which would bring up a whole new bunch of problems.

chapter 9

Dear Dr. Maude,

I don't have a lot of time to write, but I just wanted to pass along a good piece of advice that I think might be very interesting to your viewers and readers. (You know, the readers of your website and books—not the ones who you e-mail back after they e-mail you directly, because I don't think that actually ever happens.)

The advice is this: If you're ever confused as to what you should do about something, try praying for a sign. If you're not sure how you feel about God, that's okay, because what you can do is just pray to a doorknob, and it'll still totally work.

The reason I know this is because that's what I did, and I didn't just get one sign, but TWO, like one after another. But make sure to tell your fans that if they're thinking of kneeling when they pray, they might want to think about putting a blanket or a towel underneath their knees. Otherwise, they'll get sore.

In case you were wondering (not that you were, because if that was the case, you would've probably written back and asked), I had asked for signs about whether I should (a) tell Beatrice that I might-but-am-not-definitely-sure have a crush on her brother, and (b) ask him to the Sadie Hawkins dance. And they came! Like I said, I don't have a lot of time to write at the moment because now I have to actually go ask him.

Anyway, feel free to share that advice with your fans. You don't even have to say that it came from me, although it would be really nice if you did. So that you're not being a plagiarizer.

yours truly,
LUCY B. PARKER

P.S. Sorry if I'm being a little cranky with those comments about how you never write me back. I think I'm very PMS-y at the moment. At least I'm hoping I am.

If I wasn't PMS-y when I wrote the letter, and my period wasn't about to arrive any second, then I'm pretty sure it was as I made my way down to the tenth floor to launch Operation Ask Blair. With every floor number, I got more and more nervous. And more and more nauseated. By the time the doors opened up, I was worried I was going to throw up all over myself, which would NOT have been good, seeing that, for luck, Laurel had let me borrow her robin's-egg-blue cashmere sweater that I loved so much.

I made my way down the hall to Beatrice's apartment, and I thought of everything that could go wrong. Like, say, when I opened my mouth to ask him, I ended up crying. Or choking. Or not being able to open my mouth *at all* because all my nervousness would have paralyzed me to the point where I just stood there like a statue until finally I was rushed to the hospital in an ambulance.

Or, if I did manage to ask him, he laughed in my face. And then rushed over to his computer to log on to Facebook and post "Blair Lerner-Moskovitz was just asked to a dance by Lucy B. Parker and now can't stop laughing because her thinking I'd say yes is the dumbest thing in the entire world" as his status update.

I buzzed the buzzer. I had to hold on to the molding around the door in order to keep myself from running away. I had just come up with the perfect excuse to leave—I had remembered that I had left my desk lamp on by mistake and I needed to rush upstairs and turn it off so I didn't waste any more electricity—when Beatrice opened the door.

"He's not here," she announced.

"But you said he was!" I looked down at my sweater. "I got changed and everything."

"Well, he was here when I texted you, but he just went over to Larry's." Larry was Blair's BFF. According to Beatrice, Larry was even more gross than Blair, but I wasn't sure what that meant on account of the fact that

I didn't think Blair was that gross. She shook her head. "And I can't believe you dressed up for this. It's a total waste of Laurel's clothes." She squinted. "And you put real lip gloss on, too? Not just Lip Smackers?"

I swiped at my lips to wipe it off. "You promised you wouldn't keep saying stuff like this!" I cried. Talk about making a person feel embarrassed.

"Okay, okay," she agreed. "So you want to come in and hang out?"

I shook my head. "No. I want to go upstairs and take off this sweater so I don't ruin it. And wash this gunk off my lips. I'll text you later."

When I got back upstairs, I changed into sweatpants and Mom's old Smith sweatshirt, which is where she went to college. It was old, and a bit holey (not, like, in a religious way, but in a bunch-of-holes kind of way) but super-soft and comfy. After scrubbing the lip gloss off, I started my homework.

As I tried to stay awake while reading about the industrial revolution (I'm sorry, but a lot of history was *really* boring), my phone buzzed. *He's back. But he's leaving again in a few minutes for karate. I'll text u when I'm back from piano*, Beatrice had written.

Once when I was overlistening, I heard Mom tell Alan that with all the extracurricular activities that Blair and Beatrice did, she bet their moms had to take out a second mortgage on the apartment. I wasn't sure what that meant, and obviously, I couldn't ask because just the day before that I had gotten in trouble for overlistening as Mom talked on the phone to Deanna about how the women in her Pilates class had had so much plastic surgery that their faces didn't move.

Knowing that if I didn't ask Blair to the dance right then, I'd probably chicken out completely, I rushed out to the hall, not even bothering to change my clothes. And then, when the elevator didn't come, I even took the stairs. By the time I got down all eleven flights and rang the buzzer, it was hard to catch my breath.

"Hey," Blair said when he opened the door. As was always the case, he was wearing a food-stained T-shirt, this one with what looked like a pie with a piece missing that said Pac-Man underneath it. If we *did* end up going to the dance together, I wondered if it would be rude if I asked him if he could wear something nonstained. "Beatrice isn't here. She just left for piano."

"I know," I panted. "I'm not here to see her."

"You're not?" he asked suspiciously. "Well, who are you here to see then?"

I slunk down behind the door. Great. I hadn't even gotten to the asking part and already this was completely humiliating. "Umm . . . you?" I mumbled.

It kind of looked like Blair turned a little red. But then I decided it was just that my vision was screwed up from not having any air in my lungs.

"Well, come in then," he said gruffly, moving aside.

I tried to move, but my purple Converses felt like

they were glued to the floor. I looked up at the ceiling. "Really? You got me this far, and now You're pulling this?" I mumbled.

"Who are you talking to?"

"No one," I replied quickly.

"Well, are you coming in or not?"

Jeez, he really wasn't making this easy. Finally, I managed to move my legs and shuffled inside the foyer.

"So what is it?" he asked. Why was he looking at me funny? Was he psychic? Did he know what I was going to ask him?

"Oh wow—look at this!" I said, pointing to a framed playbill from a play called *A Woman's Worth,* written by Beatrice and Blair's mother Marsha. "I never noticed this before!" Okay, so maybe that was a bit of a lie. Maybe I had noticed it the very first time I had been there, and every time since then on account of the fact that the colors on it—red, green, and yellow—were so bright you almost needed sunglasses. As Blair stood there staring at me, I stood there staring at the playbill.

Finally, I turned to him. "Why are you looking at me weird?" I asked suspiciously.

"It's just . . . you have . . ." He motioned to his face.

I rolled my eyes. "You think I'm going to fall for that again?" When we were shooting my campaign video, Blair had tried to fool me with the whole you-have-a-booger-hanging-from-your-nose thing. Back then I fell for it, but now? No way.

He shrugged. "Okay. So what do you want?"

"I, uh, have a question for you," I began nervously.

He waited for me to go on, but I just stood there. Maybe I was having some sort of allergic reaction to my nervousness that was making my tongue swell up.

"I don't mean to sound like a jerk, but I'm missing the *Best Moments in Slasher Movie History* special on MTV right now," he said.

"Okay, okay." Before I began, I snuck a glimpse of myself in the mirror. Only to discover that I had gobs of zit cream dotted all over my face. I had completely forgotten I had put some on when I changed into the sweats. The good news was things couldn't get worse than this. I was absolutely, positively 175 percent humiliated. "Just so you know, this isn't zit cream," I said. "It's . . . sour cream. It's good for your skin. I learned it from Laurel. Anyway, the question is . . ." I took a deep breath. "Do you like the hot pretzels from the cart at the corner of Broadway and Eightieth, or the ones from the one at Eighty-fourth and Columbus?"

He looked confused. "You came all the way down here to ask me *that*?"

"Well, yeah. That, and . . . uh, remember Pete told you that we have a dance coming up at our school?"

He rolled his eyes. "Yes. Beatrice hogged the entire dinner conversation last night talking about it. Who wants to talk about a school dance when they had just done live brain surgery on *America's Grossest Operations*? At least that's educational."

Not to mention *disgusting*. "Yeah, well, the reason I'm bringing it up is because I was thinking of going. You know, because of the president thing. Not because I *want* to go or anything like that, because I think it's stupid, too. But because I feel like if I don't, people might get the wrong idea and impeach me."

He nodded. "That makes sense."

"So do you want to?" I asked nervously. It was a really good thing I had put a minipad over the maxipad I was wearing because I just knew I was getting my period from the stress.

"Do I want to what?" he asked, confused.

"Go with me," I replied, mopping my forehead with my sleeve. It was also a good thing I was wearing a ratty old sweatshirt rather than Laurel's expensive sweater. *Please—whatever you do, don't start bloversharing*, I thought to myself. *You said what you needed to say. Now just be quiet.* I looked down. "It's not like I want to go with you because I have a crush on you or anything like that," I blurted, "but I just thought because we're neighbors, asking you would be a nice neighborly thing to do. And because it would conserve energy," I babbled.

"How would it conserve energy?" he asked, confused.

I shrugged. "I don't know. I just know it will," I said firmly, biting my lip so hard to shut myself up that I was surprised I didn't draw blood. "*Ouch.* So do you want to go?" I demanded.

"To the dance?"

Was he making it hard for me on *purpose*? I bet he was. Maybe Beatrice was right. Maybe he was too annoying to have a crush on. "*Yes*. To the dance."

"When is it?"

"This Friday."

"I'd like to—"

"Really?!" I yelped. Wow. Who knew everyone was right about that whole you'll-never-know-unless-you-ask thing! I sure hope Anxious followed my advice, because if she did, and it worked out like this was working out, I'd be the best advice giver in the world!

"—but I can't. It's the finals of the Chess Club tournament."

"Oh. Okay," I said as my neck disappeared into my sweatshirt like a turtle. *Pleasedon'tstartcrying, pleasedon'tstartcrying*, I thought to myself. The fact that Blair had said he would have liked to should have made me really happy, but instead I found myself feeling like I was going to burst into tears. Why was I so upset? I mean, it's not like I really *wanted* to go.

And if Laurel was right about this stuff, then technically, I was a hero because I had done something that I had been afraid to do. "Well, I just remembered that I left my desk lamp on and I need to go turn it off so I don't waste energy," I mumbled. "So I'll see you around." If I could just make it to the elevator, I could cry as soon as I got in there.

"All right. See you," he said. At least that's what I

thought he said, but I was running so fast it was hard to hear.

But when the doors closed, I was too embarrassed to cry. Sure, he *said* he would have liked to go, but who knew if he really meant it? What else was he going to say? He may have been annoying, like Beatrice said, but he wasn't mean, and only a mean person would say, "Why would you ever think I'd want to go anywhere with you?" which was what he was REALLY thinking.

I may not have had to worry about asking Blair to the dance anymore, but now I had a bigger problem: how to get Mom and Alan to agree to move to Brooklyn, because there was NO WAY I could keep living in Manhattan and risk running into Blair.

chapter 10

Dear Dr. Maude,

I'm too upset at the moment to do much other than eat this entire bag of peanut-butter-filled pretzels that I've snuck into my room, but I did want you to know one thing and it's this: Don't bother giving your fans advice to pray because it turns out it doesn't work.

I mean, yes, it works in that if you pray, you'll get signs, but just because you get signs you're supposed to do something doesn't mean that things will turn out the way you want them to. So if you tell them to pray, make sure they tell whoever they're praying to, to please only give them a sign IF THINGS ARE GOING TO WORK OUT IN A GOOD WAY. Because if they're going to work out in a bad way—which is what just happened to me—then they shouldn't bother going through all the trouble.

Instead, they should just stay in their room and eat peanut-butter-filled pretzels and watch television, which is what I'm going to do with my life from now on.

I hope you're having a great day. Because I'm sure not.

yours truly,
LUCY B. PARKER

The good news about fristers is that they have to sit there and listen to you moan "I can't BELIEVE I made such a fool out of myself!" over and over, no matter how many times you need to do it. It's in the frister handbook, or would be if there was one, which was something Laurel and I were talking about writing together.

"For what it's worth, I think what you did this afternoon was amazing," she said. That was something else they had to do—cheer you up by saying nice things. "And even if it didn't work out, I bet you get some good karma from it."

"You already said that," I replied glumly.

"I did?"

"Yeah. Three times."

"Oh. Well, that's because I mean it," she said, reaching underneath her sweater to take out a box of granola bars and a bottle of Hershey's chocolate syrup. Not only did fristers have to listen to you, but they had to sneak junk food into your room. Even if only an hour before your mother told you that if she finds out you've been eating in your bedroom again when number 5 in the Parker-Moses Family Rule Book is "No eating outside of the kitchen, or—during Family TV Viewing Quality Time—living room," you'll be in big, big trouble. *And* they have to lend you their rhinestone barrette in the shape of a butterfly the next morning because it's so sparkly, and everyone knows that when a person is sad, junk food and sparkly things are the only things that can cheer them up.

But in this case, junk food and sparkly things didn't do the trick. I spent the whole week depressed. My friends tried to cheer me up ("If you want, I'll text you a lot during the dance," offered Alice) but even the way Beatrice didn't say one obnoxious thing about Blair didn't make me feel better.

"You need to promise me something, Zig," I said into the computer on Thursday afternoon as I chowed down on fried plantains and he chowed down on his arm. "When you're old enough to be asked to dances, you need to make sure you say yes. Even if you don't like the girl, okay?"

The *meh-meh-meh* sound he made obviously meant, "Of course, Lucy. I'll do whatever you want me to do because you're my big sister, which means you obviously know best."

"Because asking a boy to a dance is *hard*," I continued.

"I feel really bad for you, being a boy and all." I swear, at that he nodded, even if Dad said his neck muscles weren't strong enough for him to do that yet. "Maybe by the time you get older, it'll be more common for girls to ask boys out other than just for Sadie Hawkins dance." Before I could repeat the whole humiliating story to Ziggy (for some reason, I seemed to feel a little—not a lot, but a little—better every time I told it), there was a knock at my door.

"Come in," I called out.

Alan walked in wearing a safari-looking outfit like the guys on *Mutual of Omaha's Wild Kingdom*. "I just wanted to show you my latest purchase," he said excitedly. "Isn't it great?"

Okay, this was getting a little out of control.

"And I was thinking, in order to make the whole thing even more of a surprise, I might move the whole thing up a weekend—"

Correction: this was getting *a lot* out of control. Moving things up a weekend? It was time to come clean about how all the advice my parents thought was brilliant had really screwed things up. I couldn't let it go on anymore.

I sighed. "Alan, I think I'd like to call an Emergency Family Meeting."

A few minutes later, I found myself pacing around the living room as Mom and Alan watched from the couch. I really wanted Laurel to be there for moral support, but the idea of waiting for her to get home from the studio made me feel worse than if I just did it without her.

"Okay, there's something I need to tell you guys," I said nervously.

Mom sighed. "Is it time for us to get you a math tutor?"

"No. It's—"

"Are someone's parents suing over some advice you gave?" Alan asked anxiously.

"No." But it got me wondering—could your own parents sue you? I sure hoped not, because between all the art supplies I had bought for my campaign and my maxipad collection, I was broke. "It's about your anniversary. I know how important it is to both of you that it ends up being a special weekend."

"Oh, it is going to be special," Alan said. He turned to Mom and smiled. "Just wait till you see what I have planned for you."

She laughed. "I bet it's not as great as what *I* have planned." She glanced at him and looked puzzled. "Alan, what on earth are you wearing?"

In the drama of the Emergency Family Meeting being called, Alan had forgotten to change out of his safari outfit.

"Here's the thing," I continued. "If I don't get this out, your anniversary is actually going to be awful. See, it turns out that you both asked me for advice—"

Alan turned to Mom, confused. "You asked her, too?"
She nodded.

"—and I was really flattered when you both decided to take it. But I guess I didn't think it out very well because, see, if you follow my advice, you'll be in different states that weekend."

They looked even more confused. "Lucy, what are you talking about?" Mom asked.

"I screwed up," I admitted. "See, Mom, Alan wants to take you to this cute little bed-and-breakfast place in Vermont—"

She turned to him. "But you hate cute little bed-and-breakfasts in the country!"

"I know, but you don't," he replied. "You love them. And because I love *you*, I want to make you happy."

She took his cheeks between her hands. "Oh honey . . . that's so sweet of you!"

"I know. It is, isn't it?" he replied.

"But wait, there's more," I said. "And Alan, Mom went ahead and booked a hotel downtown and got tickets for you guys for a play—"

"Not just a play. A *musical*," Mom corrected.
He gasped. "You did?!"

She nodded. "Not only that, but I also downloaded the original-cast-recording sound track for you."

Alan looked like he was going to cry. "But, Rebecca, you hate musicals—"

She nodded. "I certainly do. But because I love you, I'll gladly suffer through one."

They looked at me. "So, Lucy, what's the problem?" Alan asked.

"'What's the *problem*?'" I cried. "The problem is I totally screwed things up! You both did the same thing, only it wasn't the same thing, and you can't do both things at once!"

Alan thought about it. "No you didn't. We'll just rearrange the schedules! I told you I was thinking of moving the Vermont weekend up, so we'll go to Vermont one weekend and spend the next one at the hotel downtown."

"It will be an extended anniversary!" Mom said excitedly. She turned to him. "I can't believe how lucky I am to have found such a thoughtful partner," she cooed as she wrapped her arms around his neck.

Okay, this was getting gross.

He put his arms around her waist. "Not as lucky as I am," he cooed back.

And now it was grosser. "Well, I guess we're done here," I said. "I'm going to go to my room now, if that's okay."

They were too busy staring into each other's eyes to notice as I walked away.

A little later there was another knock at my door.

"Lucy? Can I come in?" Alan asked.

"Mmmffssseeec," I said which was Full Mouthese for "Just a second." Great. Not only was he coming to tell me he had realized I was average, but I was going to get in trouble for eating a candy bar in my room. Just as I managed to stash the wrapper under my pillow, the door opened.

"Lucy?" he said, still wearing his safari outfit, because Mom had told him he looked handsome in it. "Sweetie, have you been crying?"

Great. I couldn't even do *that* right. "No," I lied. As soon as I said it, I realized that now was not the time to be playing around with my karma. "Okay, fine. *Yes*," I sniffled.

He grabbed my arm. "What's the matter? Is it the cramps? Did you finally get your period?" he asked anxiously.

This was so embarrassing. Why did I have to live in a family where everyone told everyone everything? More tears came. "*No.*" You would've thought that with the day I was having, the universe could've been a little nice and brought it on, but no such luck. I had even gone and checked a bunch of times to be sure.

"Then what is it?"

I tried to stop myself from crying more, but I couldn't. "It's just . . . I just . . . you just . . ." I sniffled.

"Lucy, what is it?"

"I know you're disappointed in me because I'm not talented and I don't have hobbies, so that's why I became an advice columnist, but even though I'm kind of good at it, I still managed to screw it up!" I blurted out.

"What? Why would you think I was disappointed in you?!" he asked. "And who said you're not talented?"

I wiped my nose with my sleeve. I didn't care that it was gross. "Because if I don't have any hobbies, I won't get into a good college, and then I won't get a good job. And if I don't get a good job, I won't have any money. And if I don't have any money, I'll have to live with you and Mom *forever*. Even when I'm really old. Like *fifty*." I thought about it. "But if I'm fifty, that'll mean you guys will be *really* old—like so old you'll almost be dead!" I wailed as a fresh batch of tears began coming down.

Alan sat down on the bed and pulled me into a hug. "Lucy, you have a long time before you even have to think about college. You don't need to worry about that stuff now."

"But you're always talking about it."

He sighed. "I do talk about it a lot, huh?"

I nodded into his shoulder. "Yeah. Like it's the most important thing in the world."

"I'm sorry. I guess I'm doing what my parents did to me. Which, when I think about it, is not a good thing to do because when I was your age, it used to drive me crazy, too."

I looked at him. "But you went to the best college in the world," I sniffled. Alan had gone to Harvard. Once when I was overlistening to Dad and Sarah, Dad said that even though everyone *said* Harvard was the best college in the world, it was actually overrated and that Hampshire, where he went, was a lot more fun, but I didn't think now was the time to bring that up.

He shrugged. "Yeah, and I'm very lucky to have gone there, but when I look back, I wish I had gone somewhere else."

"How come?"

"Because all I did was study so I could keep up. Study and *worry* that I wasn't going to be able to keep up." He sighed. "It wasn't a lot of fun for me."

Huh. Maybe *that's* why Alan was such a worrier and got clammy hands all the time—because he went to such a good college. He tipped my chin up toward him. "I don't care where you end up going to college. You can go to a community college for all I care," he said. "Not that that would be my first choice," he quickly added. "But the important thing is you girls are happy. That's all I care about."

"Yeah, well, when you've got so much talent like Laurel does, you don't have to worry about being happy," I said. "She's more talented at being a Regular Girl than I am, and I *am* a plain old average Regular Girl."

"Lucy, there's nothing plain or average about you," he said. "So maybe your coordination isn't so great. And maybe your singing voice isn't that terrific. And maybe you won't be at the top of the honor roll—"

I cringed. "Okay. You can stop now. I get it."

"*But* when it comes to courage, and kindness, and humor, and creativity, you're off the charts."

"You really think that?" I asked.

He shook his head. "Nope."

I slumped.

"I don't think it—I *know* it. And so does anyone else who has the honor of knowing you. Sure, Laurel may be considered a superstar by the press, but you, Lucy B. Parker, are just as much a superstar as she is. And I am beyond lucky and grateful to be your frather."

Similar to "frister," "frather" was the word I had come up with for stepfather.

My eyes filled with tears again. "Alan?"

"What?"

"I really appreciate you saying that. But you're going to have to stop because we're out of Cold Care Kleenex so I need to stop crying now."

He laughed and hugged me. Even though physical strength definitely wasn't one of my talents, I hugged back as hard as I could. Which, from the way he said, "Lucy, sweetie, you're about to break my ribs," made me think was pretty hard.

I knew a lot of kids got really bummed out when their parents got divorced. Especially if their stepparents ended up being mean. As for me, I considered it one of the best things that had happened in my life. Because not only did I have Mom and Dad, but I got Laurel and Alan and Ziggy and Sarah, too, because of it.

Even though Alan had cleared up the whole Lucy-is-so-untalented-I'm-not-sure-what-to-do-with-her issue, it didn't mean that I was suddenly all happy. Well, I was for the rest of the night. But the next day, when I woke up and realized that all my friends were going to the dance that night and I wasn't, I got sad again. Even the idea of the *Hoarders* marathon didn't cheer me up.

And when Mom told me that, as their IBS that week, she and Laurel were going to go to a special show at the Hayden Planetarium that evening, I got even more bummed out. It's not like I wanted to go—as far as I was concerned, astronomy was almost as boring as math—but it made me feel like Alan and I were the only two people on the planet who wouldn't be out doing something. Even Rose, who usually spent her Friday nights in her apartment in Queens catching up on all the soap operas she TiVo'd, was going to be out, at a church social.

As I walked into the apartment, out of breath because I still insisted on taking the stairs to avoid Blair, I knew right away something was going on.

"Um, what's going on here?" I called out nervously. Not only had the furniture been moved around so there was a bunch of wide-open space, but there was some weird-looking mirrored ball hanging from the ceiling so that the walls were covered with little sparkly reflections. Sure, I liked sparkly things, but this was A LOT of sparkle. Like give-a-person-a-headache amount of sparkle.

Alan, who was dressed in a suit and tie, looked up from the CD player and smiled. "Well, since it's just the two of us tonight . . . and seeing that you're not going to the Sadie Hawkins dance, I thought we could have a Lucy B. Parker one instead."

I looked around the room. There was a tray with cheese and crackers, and a punch bowl with two cups next to it. There was even a "Welcome to the Lucy B.

Parker Dance" poster propped up in the corner with bubble letters done by Laurel (yet another talent of hers). My eyes filled with tears. "You did all this for me?" I whispered.

"Yes, but it wasn't supposed to make you cry!" he said anxiously. "It was supposed to make you happy!" He began to pace. "This isn't good. Maybe we should call your mother. Do you want to talk to your mother?!" he babbled. Even though we weren't technically related, I was beginning to think that maybe I got my babbling from him.

I wiped my eyes. "No. It *is* making me happy," I wailed. Even though Alan could be kind of weird and annoying, this was one of the nicest things anyone had ever done for me.

"Then why are you crying?!"

"I don't know," I sniffled.

He nodded. "It's puberty. It must be puberty," he said nervously. "I remember when Laurel started with the crying. For a while there it was all day, every day. *Oy*, this is not going to be fun."

Great. Big boobs and nonstop tears. What more could a girl want? Except, you know, her *period*, which, for some reason was refusing to come.

"If you want, we could do something else. Like . . . go through the pantry and check the expiration dates."

"No. We can have the dance," I replied. Sure, on

the surface it seemed a little—okay, a lot—dorky. I mean, I hadn't wanted to go to the dance in the first place, and the idea of dancing with my frather felt kind of sad, even if I knew for a fact that because he showered twice a day he wouldn't smell, but how could I say no? He had gone to all this trouble for *me*. Maybe we weren't related by blood, but it was the kind of thing you'd do for someone who was your birth daughter. And who you loved even if she didn't have any hobbies.

He pointed at my jeans and T-shirt. "You want to wear that? Or you want to change?"

"Into what?"

"A dress? Isn't that what girls usually wear to dances?"

I shrugged. "I guess so." The truth is, I didn't want to—in fact, just a few minutes before I had been thinking of putting on Mom's holey Smith sweatshirt—but seeing that Alan was wearing a suit, which was something, like Dad, he barely ever did, it would be the polite thing to do.

I walked into my room to find my favorite dress of Laurel's—a turquoise minidress made of silk and velvet—lying on my bed with a note. "Have a great time tonight at your 'dance.' Love, Laurel." I smiled. Not only did I have the best frather in the world—I had the best frister.

A few minutes later I walked out into the living room

wearing the dress with my favorite brown cowboy boots. "Oh Lucy, you look beautiful!" Alan exclaimed.

"I do?" I asked. Because it was just Alan and me, I hadn't bothered to brush my hair or put on lip gloss or anything. He picked up his camera. "Let me take some shots so we can show your mom and Laurel."

"Okay," I shrugged. Usually when a person had pictures taken of them at a dance, it was a dance that wasn't happening in their living room, and there was a boy in the picture with them, but because Alan didn't know how to use the self-timer on his camera, the photos were just of me.

"And let's do one over here, by the window," he said a few minutes later. "Try and look . . . serious. As if you're thinking about the mysteries of the universe."

"But aren't dances supposed to be fun?" I asked, confused.

He thought about it. "Yes. I guess. Because I only went to one when I was growing up, I don't know a lot about them, but you're right, in the movies they always are."

"You only went to one dance?" I asked. I hadn't known that.

He nodded. "Yes. My senior prom. At the very last minute. With my second cousin Barbara, who was in town from Chicago."

Huh. Maybe taking relatives to these things wasn't as

weird as I had thought. I wish I had some boy cousins. That would make the next few years a lot easier. "Was that because you were studying so hard to get into Harvard?" I asked.

He nodded. "But my mother was afraid that if I graduated without having attended one dance, it might affect me psychologically for the rest of my life, so she made me take Barbara," he said.

"Did you have a good time?" I asked.

He shook his head. "No. Fifteen minutes into it she went off with Craig Spencer, and I spent the entire evening alone at my table. And this was before BlackBerrys and cell phones, so I couldn't even pretend to be busy checking my e-mail. Not that I would have gotten a lot back then."

Wow. Poor Alan. I had always guessed he was a little weird growing up, but I hadn't known he was *that* unpopular. For some reason, it made me love him even more. No wonder why, back when I was running for president, he had thought that my promise to stop the division between the Haves and the Have-Nots was such a good one.

"And the reason I decided to have this dance was so that your childhood could be a little different than mine," he said. "I know it's not a *real* dance, and I know I'm just your frather. Well, not even your frather because your mom and I aren't married yet . . . which would instead make me your . . ." He thought about it. "I'm not sure what that would make me."

"It makes you my *frather*," I replied with a smile. "Whether you're married or not."

He started to get teary. "Oh, Lucy—that makes me so happy."

Uh-oh. When Alan got emotional, sometimes it was very hard to calm him down. "Yup. You're my frather. So, uh, we should probably get this dance thing started," I said.

He walked over to the CD player and pushed a button. As sappy music filled the room, he walked over to me and held out his arm. "May I have this dance?"

I shrugged. "I guess so."

As he led me out into the dance floor, or, as most people would call it, the area near the TV where the coffee table usually was, we started dancing. If stepping all over someone's feet and bumping into them could be considered "dancing."

"I know you're disappointed that you're not at the dance tonight," he said. "But there will be other ones. I promise."

I looked up at him. "But how do you know?"

"I just know." He smiled. "I'm a frather—we know about these things."

I smiled back and went back to stepping all over

his feet. "Is this that Neil Diamond guy?" I asked after a moment. Neil Diamond was this sappy old-time singer who Alan loved. In fact, the second time the four of us ever went out—to karaoke—he picked a song by him to sing.

"It sure is. I think it's perfect dance music, don't you?"

Because of the never-having-been-to-a-dance thing, I wasn't positive, but I was pretty sure that, no, it was not. "And who's the woman singing with him?" I asked.

"Barbra Streisand," he replied excitedly.

The name sounded familiar. In fact, I was pretty sure my grandmother had a bunch of CDs by that woman.

"It's called 'You Don't Bring Me Flowers,'" he said. "It's a real classic. Perfect for dancing."

As we bumped around a little more, I looked up at him. "But when you listen to the words, it's a little sad, isn't it?" I asked. "I mean, they're saying things like you don't sing me love songs, and you barely talk to me anymore . . ."

He thought about it. "Yes, now that I think about it, I guess you're right," he agreed. "Oh my God. It's so depressing! How did I not realize how depressing this song was! It's got a great melody, but you're right, the words are just . . ." He ran over to the CD player and turned it off as he started hunting through his CD collection. "We could listen to . . . no, this one is depressing, too . . . what about . . . no, this one is only good if you're going through a breakup . . ."

"Um, Alan?"

He turned to me. "Yeah?"

"This dance thing is great. Really. It's like one of the nicest things anyone has ever done for me," I said. "But I was wondering . . . would it be okay if we just, I don't know, went and got some ice cream instead?"

"You're sure? Because I really wanted you to have the whole dance experience." He held up a bowl. "I even went as far as to put together a raffle."

For some reason, that made me start crying again. It was just so . . . sweet. Really, really corny, but completely sweet.

"Oh no! You're crying again! Please don't cry," he said anxiously. "We don't have to do the raffle. Of course we can go for ice cream."

"We can?" I sniffled.

He nodded. "Yes. You can even get a sundae if you want."

"With extra hot butterscotch?"

"Yes. But don't tell your mother. Go get your coat."

As I walked over to the closet, I smiled.

The night was turning out a lot better than I thought it would. In fact, there was nothing else I'd rather be doing.

Before we walked out the door, I stopped and began to rummage through my new tote bag with a map of Manhattan on it. "Hold on," I said. "I just need to write something down." I took out my advice notebook and purple pen: "When you have the guts to be honest and do things that scare you—whether it's ask a boy to a dance or tell your parents you kind of screwed up—things have a way of working out exactly as they're supposed to. Complete with ice cream sundaes."

chapter 11

Dear Dr. Maude,

For someone who said she wasn't going to write to you anymore, I sure do write you a lot, huh?

Anyway, I don't need advice at this moment in time, but I did want to give you some. So you can pass it along to your fans. And the advice is this: Try not to get too upset about things, because the truth is, you never know what's going to happen.

Alan and I had a talk on Thursday night, and it turns out that he's okay with the fact that I don't have any hobbies. He says that I'm talented in other ways, like in my Lucyness. And then on Friday night, he put together this whole fake dance for him and me, which was really corny but very sweet. Because he chose this sad song by Neil Diamond for us to dance to, it kind of killed the mood, and because of my coordination issues, I ruined his shoes because I kept stepping on his feet. Which is why we just ended up going for ice cream instead of dancing. But when we got home, this e-mail was waiting for me:

To: lucy

From: blair

Subject: not sure

    Hey Lucy. It's Blair. From downstairs. Sorry I couldn't go to that dance thing with you tonight. Anyway, I was wondering . . . Maybe you want to go do something at some point. Together. Or not. I don't really care either way. But I thought because you asked me to that dance thing, I would ask. Anyway, bye.

I'll have to go over it with Laurel in the morning to figure out what it really means, but if you ask me, it kind-of-sort-of sounds like he's asking me to do something with him, don't you think? Or maybe not. I'm not totally sure.

Either way, I don't feel so bad right now. Although if he IS asking me to do something, then I'll have to hang out with him. Which could make me very nervous. And possibly bring my period on. Which would be both good and bad at the same time.

As for the whole advice-giving business, it looks like I'm staying in it. At least for a while. Dr. Rem-Wall called me into her office yesterday and said that she wanted me to tell Annie that because of the overwhelmingly positive response from some of the parents, she wanted to extend my contract for six months. I didn't even know I had a contract! Isn't that amazing? Here I was thinking

I had totally screwed up, but people—not just kids, but PARENTS—like what I'm doing.

Laurel says that now's the time to talk to her agent about the idea of me pitching an advice talk show to different TV networks, but I said I wasn't interested. Mostly because even though you don't write me back, I feel a lot of loyalty toward you, and if my show went on to be supersuccessful, that would probably hurt your feelings.

There is one big change, though. Because I'm now big on this whole honesty thing, I told Dr. Rem-Wall that Annie was actually me, or I'm actually Annie, or whatever the right way to say that is. For some reason she didn't seem so surprised, which was weird. So starting next week, the column will now be called "Ask Lucy B. Parker." I'm a little nervous about giving advice as Lucy rather than Annie, but Laurel says that if I just speak from the heart, I'll be fine.

I sure hope so. Obviously, I'll keep you posted.

Even though you don't write me back.

yours truly,
LUCY B. PARKER

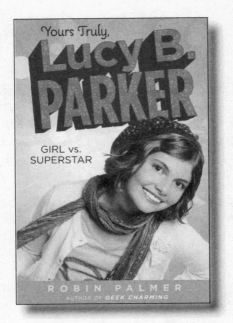

1: Girl vs. Superstar

Sixth grade is hard enough for Lucy B. Parker, but it gets so much worse when her mom announces that she's going to marry Laurel Moses's dad. Yes, *that* Laurel Moses—the tv-movie-music star. All Lucy wants is to just get through the day without totally embarrassing herself, but that's hard to do when you're the less-pretty, less-talented not-quite-sister of a mega superstar.

978-0-14-241500-9

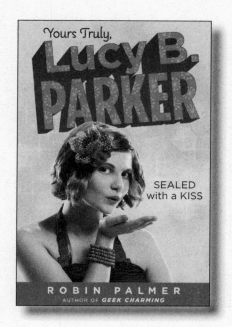

2: Sealed with a Kiss

Lucy B. Parker is spending her summer vacation off in L.A., visiting Laurel on the set of her new movie and meeting teen heartthrobs left and right. Life is good, until Lucy develops a crush—and unlike previous crushes, this one is not on a character in a book or a movie, but on a real living, breathing boy. Unfortunately for Lucy, nothing ever seems to go as she plans.

978-0-14-241501-6

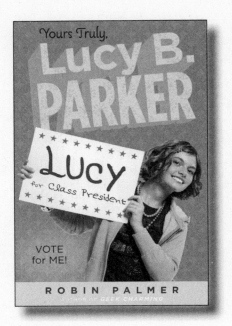

3: Vote for Me!

Lucy B. Parker is running for class president! And she's up against the most popular girl in school. Sure, Lucy could let her frister (friend + sister), teen superstar Laurel Moses, campaign for her, but Lucy wants to win as *Lucy*. How is Lucy going to manage the campaign of the year?

978-0-14-241502-3

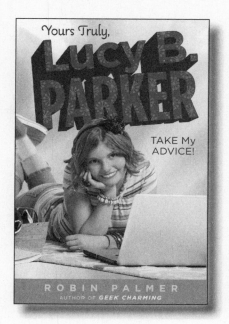

Yours Truly,

LUCY B. PARKER

TAKE My ADVICE!

ROBIN PALMER

AUTHOR OF *GEEK CHARMING*

4: Take My Advice!

When Lucy becomes the advice columnist for her school paper, she suddenly has a lot more on her plate than she bargained for. Lucy's not really sure how she's going to pull this off, but with the Sadie Hawkins dance coming up, it seems like everyone in her class needs some help.

978-0-14-241503-0

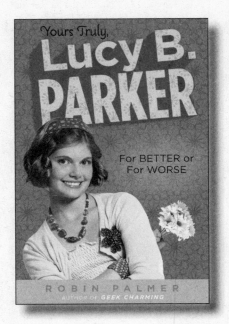

5: For Better or For Worse

When Lucy's mom and soon-to-be stepdad announce that they're finally getting married—in a month—Lucy's life turns upside down. Wedding planning is hard enough, but when a reality TV crew ends up following the family around while it's happening, the results are disastrous. Can Lucy save the day—not to mention, the family—or will everything fall apart?

978-0-14-241504-7

Get Hooked
ON THESE OTHER
FABULOUS
Girl Series!

Lucy B. Parker: Girl vs. Superstar
By Robin Palmer
AVAILABLE NOW!

Forever Four
By Elizabeth Cody Kimmel
AVAILABLE NOW!

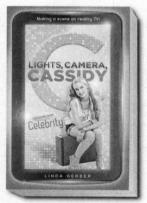

Lights, Camera, Cassidy: Episode 1: Celebrity
By Linda Gerber
Coming Soon! 3/15/2012

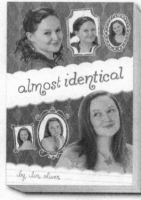

Almost Identical
By Lin Oliver
Coming Soon! 6/28/2012

**Check out sample chapters at
http://tinyurl.com/penguingirlsampler**